"What I have to say is regarding the body, er. . . Mr. Woodruff."

Using the word *body* seemed uncivilized and disrespectful.

He stood looking at her, notebook in hand and pen in his shirt pocket, clearly uninterested in her or whatever information she might have.

Pricilla held her head high. "I believe that I am the one who murdered Mr. Woodruff."

D0685165

Don't miss out on any of our great mysteries. Contact us at the following address for information on our newest releases and club information:

Heartsong Presents—MYSTERIES! Readers' Service
PO Box 721
Uhrichsville, OH 44683
Web site: www.heartsongmysteries.com

Or for faster action, call 1-740-922-7280.

Recipe for Murder

A Cozy Crumb Mystery

Lisa Harris

HEARTSONG
PRESENTS
MYSTERIES

Many thanks to my fantastic Cozy Mystery Crit Group whose watchful eyes and encouraging words helped me to bring Pricilla's story to life, and to Candy and Laurie Alice for all their awesome input. A special thank you, also, to my wonderful family and its constant cheering me on this writer's journey. And lastly, to my fearless editor, Susan Downs, for believing in me and my story.

ISBN 978-1-59789-484-5

Copyright © 2008 by Lisa Harris. All rights reserved. Except for use in any review, the reproduction or utilization of this work in whole or in part in any form by any electronic, mechanical, or other means, now known or hereafter invented, is forbidden without the permission of Heartsong Presents—MYSTERIES!, an imprint of Barbour Publishing, Inc., PO Box 721, Uhrichsville, OH 44683.

All scripture quotations, unless otherwise indicated, are taken from the HOLY BIBLE, NEW INTERNATIONAL VERSION®. NIV®. Copyright © 1973, 1978, 1984 by International Bible Society. Used by permission of Zondervan. All rights reserved.

All of the characters and events in this book are fictitious. Any resemblance to actual persons, living or dead, or to actual events is purely coincidental.

Cover design: Kirk DouPonce, DogEared Design

Our mission is to publish and distribute inspirational products offering exceptional value and biblical encouragement to the masses.

Printed in the United States of America.

Retirement was not what Pricilla Crumb envisioned. If asked, she would compare it to one of her prized cheese soufflés gone flat. Dull and disappointing. Thankfully, her son, Nathan, had been desperate enough to fly her to the upscale hunting lodge he owned, or more than likely she'd be sitting at her card table right now, putting together one of those five-hundred-piece puzzles her next-door neighbor had given her last Christmas. Filling in for Nathan's full-time cook, who had come down with a serious case of the West Nile virus four months ago, had, it seemed, become her escape from the yawning predictability of retirement.

Pricilla sorted through the stack of cookbooks piled beside her on the kitchen's granite countertop. Most of tonight's menu had been set three days ago, but a problem had arisen with the appetizer. Rendezvous, Colorado, might not be the smallest dot on the state map, but it certainly lacked some of the conveniences of Seattle, one of them being oysters, a key ingredient for her grilled oyster dish.

At least the lodge's newly remodeled kitchen left nothing to complain about. The antique-styled cabinets, professional appliances, and aged ceiling beams that added a finishing touch to the spacious room, was a chef's dream. Already, Pricilla hoped that the temporary position would become permanent. Moving back to Colorado and near her son would be worth giving up a few conveniences of the city.

Penelope, her Persian cat, paraded into the room and pressed against her legs.

"Where have you been? Hiding under the bed again?" With the top of her foot, Pricilla rubbed Penelope under the chin. "You'll have to wait a while, my sweet, unless you have an idea for the perfect starter."

She flipped through another book of appetizers then dog-eared one of the pages. Finally, she'd found something suitable. Salmon-filled tartlets would be an ideal choice start to tonight's dinner.

The timer on the oven buzzed, and Pricilla crossed the hardwood floor to check on her cake. With the weather still surprisingly warm as the calendar moved into October, the baked Alaska flambé would be the perfect ending to the meal. Presentation, as she'd always taught her students, was half the goal with food preparation, and the lighting of the meringue would be the highlight of the evening. She had seen Julia Child present the flaming dessert on television with awed reactions. Pricilla foresaw nothing less for tonight.

Nathan entered the kitchen and kissed her on the forehead, frowning when he saw the stack of cookbooks. "Mom, I thought you promised me you'd keep the menu simple tonight."

She eyed her son's tall, handsome frame before pulling

the almond and orange cake from the oven and setting it on a rack. "I haven't prepared anything I wouldn't have fixed for your father for a typical Sunday afternoon meal. Roast pork, herbed oven-roasted potatoes— "

"I admit that you're anything but a typical cook, but"—he glanced at the opened cookbook—"salmon-filled tartlets?"

"They're delicious. You'll love them." She paused, trying to remember if she'd checked the expiration date on the smoked salmon. Surely she had. It was second nature by now.

"I'm sure I will," Nathan continued, "but a simple pot roast with vegetables on the side would have been fine."

She dismissed his concerns with the wave of her hand and checked on the rising dough for her yeast rolls. "The reputation of this lodge is at stake, and I don't plan to have anything to do with tarnishing it. Which reminds me." She turned toward him, her hands placed firmly on her hips. "You must speak to the owner of the grocery store. There are a number of things they don't carry, making it quite inconvenient—"

"Mom, my regular cook never had a problem with getting what she needed." He cocked his head and shot her a smile. "I'm sure that the guests will be happy with whatever you fix. You are Pricilla Crumb, hostess and cook extraordinaire, are you not? Besides, I didn't bring you up here to work you to death. You need to relax a bit."

She couldn't help but smile back. He always knew how to appease her. Without a doubt he had her completely wrapped around his finger. She'd do anything for him, and he knew it.

"I suppose I am a bit keyed up." Pricilla rubbed her hands on her apron. "It's just with all the guests arriving in the next few hours, as well as Max and his daughter Trisha. . ." Pricilla turned back to her bowl of dough, pausing for emphasis. There was no reason to pass up an opportunity to further her plan. "Trisha's such a sweet girl. It's strange that the two of you have never met, despite all the years I've known Max." She glanced at her son.

"It is strange, isn't it?" His expression confirmed he wasn't a bit moved by her ploys of innocence. "Especially considering the fact that you've told me about her at least a half dozen times. And that's just since yesterday." Nathan leaned against the counter. "Let's see. Trisha is a graphic designer with long hair, stunning eyes, and. . . how could I forget? She's single."

Pricilla ignored her son's teasing tone. *Single* was the key word here, because she had a plan. She was certain that sparks would fly once the two of them met. With her matchmaking skills sharpened and detailed plans in place, she was convinced that Trisha Summers was the perfect antidote to her son's lonely heart.

Nathan popped a handful of walnuts into his mouth from a ceramic bowl on the counter. "Why are you so worried about me, despite the fact that I keep assuring you that I'm not lonely? I love running the lodge, meeting new people, and—"

"Running this lodge, no matter how successful, will never bring you true happiness—or give me grandchildren." There. She'd made her point.

"Okay, but what about you, Mom?" He leaned down and caught her gaze, his eyes suddenly dark and serious. "Don't you think it would be far more suitable to find someone for yourself before attempting to try and find a match for your only son?"

Pricilla frowned. That was an entirely different subject. She dropped the ball of dough onto a floured board and started kneading. "I'm not convinced life gives second chances when it comes to true love."

When her husband, Marty, died, she decided to thank the good Lord for loaning him to her for almost forty years. She'd found love once and wasn't certain she'd ever find what she had with him again. Still, while she wouldn't ever admit to anyone that she was lonely, it was hard not to wonder at times what it would be like to share her life with someone other than Penelope.

Max Summers sneaked a hot yeast roll from the bread basket, intent on avoiding Pricilla's watchful gaze. He thought the chances of her catching him, though, were slim. With all the guests here and dinner about to be served, she was running around with the precision of a military general and finishing up last-minute details. He'd rarely seen her more in her element.

"I saw you sneak that roll, Max Summers."

He sat back on the bar stool and shot her his most guilty expression. "You know I never could resist your cooking. And I'm not the only one. I just saw one of your guests steal out of the dining room with a plateful of appetizers."

"Charles Woodruff, I assume?" Pricilla frowned. "He's already complained that dinner was being served too late. Like seven o'clock is an uncivilized hour to eat."

"Do you expect all the guests to be as cantankerous as Mr. Woodruff?"

Despite the warmth of the kitchen, Pricilla's silver hair lay in perfect curls against the nape of her neck, and her face, with just a hint of makeup, still looked fresh. The years might have added a few wrinkles and age spots, but he still found her beautiful.

"It's a small crowd this week. Charles's wife, Claire, seems sweet. The quiet type, I understand, who spends most of her time reading romance novels." Pricilla pulled out another pan of hot rolls from the top oven, the heavenly smell reminding him just how hungry he was. "There are also three college buddies who return each year. Let's see, I think their names are Simon Wheeler, Anthony Mills, and Michael Smythe. Nathan told me that they're businessmen who made it big with their. . .their dot company—"

"Dot-com company." Max stifled a laugh. Pricilla knew nothing about computers. E-mail correspondence would have been the perfect way for them to keep in touch, but she insisted on the old-fashioned method, the post office.

"Anyway," Pricilla continued, "Nathan said they were among the few who managed to survive the fallout in the nineties. Apparently they sold the company a couple years ago for quite a fortune."

He watched her flutter around the kitchen and found himself worrying about her. Even with Misty, the housekeeper, helping, he knew that cooking three meals a day for all the guests and staff of the resort lodge wasn't easy.

He finished the last of his roll. "You're overdoing it, Pricilla."

Pricilla put her fists against her hips and frowned. "Why? Because I'm retired and should be sitting out on my back porch, knitting or, even better, categorizing my dozens of herbal pills and vitamins like my friend Madge?"

"I do remember that Madge's obsession with supplements was a bit extreme, but what's wrong with knitting?" Max smiled. He loved to tease her. "I can't remember my mother ever being without knitting needles in her hands."

Her eyes widened. "I wasn't trying to imply that there's anything wrong with knitting, it's just that—"

"Don't worry." This time Max didn't even try not to laugh. "I can't see you knitting either."

"Thank you. I think." Pricilla frowned and peeked into the bottom oven, letting the savory scent of marinated pork fill the room.

"It smells fantastic." Max knew she loved compliments, and he tried to hand them out freely.

"Let's hope the guests agree."

"Undoubtedly they will."

Pricilla had always been the perfect cook and hostess, and he was quite sure she missed teaching her students at the Willow Hill Private Academy for Girls how to become the same. Times had changed too much, though. Today's generation rarely cooked from scratch anymore, and formal dinners around the family table were becoming a thing of the past. The principal had insisted Pricilla retire and instead hired a girl straight out of university whose idea of a home-cooked meal was frozen lasagna from the supermarket. For Pricilla, leaving behind the academy had been like losing a part of herself.

He, on the other hand, didn't miss working. After giving thirty-five years to his country and the United States Air Force, he loved his newfound freedom. Last week he'd gone fishing four days in a row, just because he wanted to.

"Where's your daughter?" Pricilla brushed some flour off her apron, making sure it didn't get on her red pants suit, then pulled a large glass bowl out of one of the oak cabinets. "I haven't seen her since you arrived, and I'm anxious to introduce her to Nathan."

"I'm already ahead of you." Max watched her expression closely. "Introductions have been made, and the last time I peeked into Nathan's office, they were still talking."

Pricilla's eyes widened. "Really?"

"Really."

He couldn't believe he'd agreed to conspire with her in her most recent scheme to match up his business-oriented daughter with Pricilla's like-minded son. His real reason to come for the week, though, had nothing to do with his daughter's love life. He watched as Pricilla busied herself at the stove. Stirring, tasting. . .adding a bit of salt and pepper. . .then stirring some more.

Violet had been gone almost five years now, and while he still missed her, he had to admit he wouldn't mind sharing his life with someone as fun-loving as Pricilla, even if she was a bit overbearing at times. The problem was, he knew that Pricilla saw him as nothing more than a close friend. Even through their years of correspondence, that fact never changed. Still, he loved the intelligent conversations with her and wondered if perhaps God might grant him one last chance to change their relationship into something more permanent.

Someone screamed.

"What in the world—" Max jumped off the bar stool and ran out of the kitchen, with Pricilla following.

The scream had originated from the second floor of

the log-styled building. Max rushed up the staircase and down the hall, stopping at the first open door. Claire Woodruff was bent over her husband, her face paler than a December sky. Charles Woodruff sat slumped sideways in a wingback chair beside the fireplace, his face contorted and pink. A half empty plate of Pricilla's tartlets lay strewn across the stone hearth.

"It's Charles." Claire stood up to face Max, her expression void of any emotion. "I think. . .I think he's dead."

Charles Woodruff was dead, and, for all Pricilla knew, her salmon tartlets had killed him. She'd said as much to Max as she had hurried from the Woodruffs' room after seeing the body. She knew first-hand about food poisoning, though she wasn't sure how long it took for someone to succumb to death after ingesting fatal morsels. Charles couldn't have been dead longer than thirty minutes or so after eating them. She'd set the appetizers on the warmer on the buffet table, never intending that anyone eat them until dinner was announced.

"It wasn't you, Pricilla," Max said while entering the kitchen twenty minutes later.

"You don't know that." She poured extra cleanser on the counter and began scrubbing in vigorous circles. The local detective was upstairs right now doing whatever it was that the authorities did in a situation like this. She shuddered, thinking of what poor Mrs. Woodruff might be going through with her husband dying during their romantic week away in the mountains.

Max closed the distance between them and stood beside her at the counter. "Pricilla, you're upset and not thinking clearly—"

"He died eating my tartlets. The evidence was right there!" She threw the sponge into the sink. "Speaking of evidence, I'm tampering with it—"

Max grabbed her wrists and gently pulled her into a hug "This wasn't your fault. He could have had heart problems."

"Claire said he was in perfect health."

"People in the best of health often die unexpectedly. It could have been any number of things—heart attack, stroke, a ruptured aorta—"

"Stop, Max, please. How would you feel if your prized tartlets were the last thing someone ingested before he died?"

She pulled away from him, desperate for something to keep her busy while she waited for the authorities to interrogate her. Nathan was with the police, and Trisha had volunteered to stay with Claire, leaving her to fend for the other guests. She mulled over her options. She could whip up a batch of cinnamon rolls or perhaps one of her lemon crumb cakes. No. No one would want to sample her cooking after tonight.

Max leaned against the edge of the counter and caught her gaze. "I think he was fortunate to have tried some of your wonderful cooking before dying."

Pricilla turned away from him. "Max, you're absolutely impossible. Just last week I read an article about an entire family dying from salmonella poisoning. Something in the stuffed pasta shells—"

"You read too much."

"But this wasn't fiction." She shivered, and it wasn't from the drop in temperature as night descended on the mountains around them. "This really happened. . . like tonight really happened."

"Cases like that are very rare, and I simply can't imagine anything being wrong with your tartlets."

"They'll have to test them." This had her worried.

Max grabbed a glass from the cupboard and headed toward the fridge. "More than likely they will announce that Mr. Woodruff had a heart attack, and there will be no need to even test the contents of your appetizers."

"I've hidden them in the bottom of the deep freeze in a trash bag. I can't have someone else coming down for a late night snack and falling over dead."

That sudden thought bothered her. What if someone else had sampled one of her appetizers and succumbed to Mr. Woodruff's fate? On the other hand—

"Perhaps Mr. Woodruff's death was actually a blessing," she stated.

Max stopped pouring the soda into his glass and looked up at her, a surprised expression written across his face. "A blessing?"

"Of course, it's a dreadful shame for Mr. Woodruff, but what if all the guests had eaten them?" Pricilla stared out the window, where the last of the sunlight was fading beyond the mountains peaks. "One by one we all could have dropped off like flies. It would have been like some nightmare out of *And Then There Were None*—you know, one of Agatha Christie's best mysteries."

"Like I said, you've been reading too many novels, Pricilla." Max set down his glass and grabbed the kettle off the stove. "What you need is a nice, relaxing cup of tea."

Pricilla frowned as Max proceeded to fill the kettle. Her head was pounding, and she was certain her blood pressure had risen a notch or two. She'd have to remember to take her medicine tonight. Leave it to Max, with his orderly, military mind-set, to think that a cup of tea could smooth over the raw reality of death.

Nathan entered the room with Trisha right behind him.

"I've been upstairs with Detective Carter," Nathan said. "He'll want to talk to all of us. Quite routine, of course, since he believes Mr. Woodruff died from natural causes."

"Natural causes?" Pricilla's stomach churned. "How long has Detective Carter been working for the department?"

"I don't know. Six. . .eight months at the most. He's the sheriff's nephew but he seems like he knows what he's doing. Not much ever happens in Rendezvous to merit a large show of force. The sheriff is back East at a conference of some type, apparently."

Her son's comments were anything but assuring.

Nathan grabbed a handful of peanuts and popped a few in his mouth. "Are you all right, Mom? You're looking a bit pale."

"How can you be so calm about all of this, Nathan?" Pricilla felt the veins in her neck pulsate. Was she the only one taking this event seriously? "There's a dead man in one of your upstairs suites."

"Your mother thinks she poisoned Mr. Woodruff with one of her tartlets." Max took a sip of his drink.

"What?" Nathan and Trisha's simultaneous response only added to the pain of Pricilla's pounding temples.

"That's ridiculous," Nathan said.

"Completely," Max echoed. "I've been trying to convince her otherwise, but your mother's stubborn."

"I know."

Pricilla fumed. They were talking as if she weren't in the room. It was a habit that irritated her.

Nathan caught her gaze. "Does this have anything to do with Dr. Witherspoon?"

"Of course not." Pricilla clutched her stomach. "That was an entirely different situation. Dr. Witherspoon and his wife simply suffered from cramps, vomiting, and nausea. . . . Charles Woodruff is dead."

"Who's Dr. Witherspoon?" Trisha asked Pricilla.

She went back to cleaning the counters. The detective might confiscate her tartlets, but at least the kitchen would be sparkling. "He was a friend of my late husband's. We invited him and his wife over for dinner. Nathan must have been about twelve at the time. Apparently I hadn't noticed that the mayonnaise had expired. We all ended up in the emergency room for hours. It was dreadful."

Trisha covered her mouth with her hand. "Oh my, that is awful."

"Terrible," Max echoed.

Pricilla frowned. Max and Trisha were showing far too much interest in an event she would prefer to forget. "I wish Nathan hadn't brought it up. It was such a humiliating moment."

"Since then, my mother's been fanatical about checking expiration dates and making certain of where everything comes from." Nathan wrapped his arm around his mother's shoulder. "And that's the very reason why I'm certain your tartlets couldn't have been the reason for Charles Woodruff's demise."

Trisha folded her arms across her chest and frowned. "Mrs. Crumb, I can see how it's possible for that situation to make you overreact today, but the truth is, no one knows what has happened, except that Mr. Woodruff is dead. And I, for one, am certain it wasn't from your tartlets. This is nothing more than an unfortunate event that has us all on edge."

Pricilla wanted to believe Trisha—all of them, in fact—but that didn't take away the overwhelming guilt. She felt like she had when their neighbor had to drive them all to the hospital. She'd let them all down, including Nathan—and now she was afraid she'd let him down again. Not only would her reputation as a hostess and cook be ruined, but the future of Nathan's lodge could be forever tarnished because of her. No one would return to a place where the cook had killed one of the guests.

The kettle began to whistle, and Max pulled it off the burner. "I thought we could all use a cup of tea."

Pricilla busied herself pulling boxes of tea and sugar out of the cupboard. Three boxes of prepackaged cookies sat on the bottom shelf. She cringed at the thought of serving a store-bought dessert, but decided to pull them out anyway.

She turned around and watched as Trisha filled a tray with mugs. The girl was beautiful in her loose-fitting pants suit and open-toed shoes. Her hair lay in soft ringlets around her shoulders. Pricilla was certain she highlighted it, but the honey color accented her skin tone to perfection. And Trisha was also completely efficient. That was one reason Pricilla loved Trisha and knew the young woman would be perfect for her son. Already, she'd managed to help bring calm to the chaos of the evening.

But any thoughts of matchmaking had to be set aside for the time being. Pricilla knew what she must do now. The salmon had smelt funny, she was sure of it, looking back. She must not have looked at the expiration date. And the cream cheese. She couldn't be sure about that ingredient's freshness either. Why hadn't she been more careful? She of all people knew of the dangers of food poisoning. She set the tea and cookies down on the counter and cleared her throat. A hot cup of tea would never fix what had happened today.

"If you will all excuse me, there's something I must do. I'm going find the detective and confess that I poisoned Charles Woodruff."

Max stared at Pricilla, certain he'd heard her wrong.

He knew she was stubborn, but this was absurd. He was tempted to drag the rest of the tartlets out of the freezer and eat one just to prove to her that there was nothing wrong with them. Only the remote chance that she was right stopped him.

Pricilla slipped out of the room before anyone could think of something to say. Then Max set his drink down on the counter. "I'm going to try and talk some sense into that woman."

"It won't do any good, I'm afraid," Nathan said. "You know my mother. Once she gets something into her head, it's impossible to reason with her or change her mind."

Max stopped and turned around in the doorway. He noticed the circles under Nathan's eyes. Maybe his playing it cool was an act. Max didn't blame him at all for being upset, though. Having a death occur on one's premises was nerve-racking no matter what the circumstances. Max shifted his feet. "You don't think it's possible that there was something wrong with the tartlets—"

"Of course not." Nathan grabbed another handful of nuts and shook them in the palm of his hand. "I just don't know what else to say to her."

"I think I'll skip the tea for now. I'm going to see if I can do something for Claire." Trisha laid a hand on Max's shoulder. "Dad, why don't you see if you can talk some sense into Mrs. Crumb? What we don't need are rumors circulating about poisoned tartlets, so you need to convince her to keep quiet. And to not worry."

Max let out a deep sigh and nodded. That would be easier said than done.

~

Pricilla caught Detective Carter outside as he was heading toward his unmarked car. She felt her knees tremble as the gravel drive crunched beneath her shoes. Darkness had fallen, but the front of the lodge was well lit by domed lights.

"Detective, I need to speak to you regarding an urgent matter."

The detective adjusted his glasses. "I'm sorry, Miss—"

"Mrs. Pricilla Crumb."

"Mrs. Crumb, then. I am sorry, but right now I have to make arrangements for a body to be transported, and—"

"What I have to say is regarding the body, er. . .Mr. Woodruff." Using the word *body* seemed uncivilized and disrespectful.

He stood looking at her, notebook in hand and pen in his shirt pocket, clearly uninterested in her or whatever information she might have.

Pricilla held her head high. "I believe that I am the one who murdered Mr. Woodruff."

This got his attention. "Excuse me?"

"The victim, Mr. Woodruff, was in the process of

consuming one of my salmon-filled tartlets when he expired."

"Expired?"

"Passed away." Pricilla shook her head. She had no idea it would be so difficult to turn herself in.

"Mrs. . .Crumb." The bald detective shook his head. "I'm sure that you have the best intentions of helping by confessing to the crime, but I've seen situations like this dozens of times."

She didn't understand. "When the chef killed a guest?"

The man shook his head again. "No, when a man died from a heart attack."

"A heart attack."

"For now, I'm convinced that there was no foul play involved in Mr. Woodruff's death, so please don't give another thought about the. . ."

"Tartlets." The man should be taking notes.

"Tartlets. Yes. I'm certain there is nothing at all for you to worry about."

Confirmation from the law should have cleared her mind, but she couldn't be completely certain until her appetizers were tested. "Do you have a lab where they can be tested?"

He shoved his notebook in his back pants pocket. "We will take every step to find out exactly how Mr. Woodruff died, but as I said, I'm sure you have nothing to worry about in regard to your dinner. Now, if you'll excuse me. I need to head back into town."

What else could she say? More than likely, she thought cynically, the detective was trying to quickly wrap up the case to impress his uncle. She turned back to the lodge, irritated that the man had dismissed her declaration of guilt.

"Pricilla?" Max stopped her at the edge of the sidewalk as the detective peeled out of the driveway. "What did you tell the detective?"

She tried to ignore Max's intense gaze. "Simply that I was concerned my tartlets might have been involved in Mr. Woodruff's demise."

"Pricilla—"

"He told me they believed Mr. Woodruff died of natural causes."

"So are you convinced finally that you had nothing to do with the man's death?"

Pricilla bit her lip. "I need to go see if I can help Claire. She must be so upset."

"You didn't answer my question."

"I've always taken pride in my cooking, and to think that I could have poisoned someone—"

"You still aren't answering my question."

"I want them to test the appetizers. Then I can be certain."

"I suppose that's reasonable, but—"

"No buts, Max. I want—"

The shriek of the smoke alarm interrupted Pricilla.

Max's eyes widened. "Something's on fire."

He sniffed the air and dashed up the porch stairs, taking the steps two at a time.

Pricilla hurried behind Max into the house and toward the persistent blare of the smoke detector. The soles of her shoes clicked against the gray-tiled floor of the entryway as she struggled to keep up with him. The minute she entered the kitchen, she saw the thick gray cloud of smoke that poured out of the oven.

Her roast pork!

Pricilla pressed the palm of her hand against her mouth and tried not to choke on the fumes. How could she have forgotten to turn off the oven?

"Open the back door! I'll get the windows!" Max shouted.

Pricilla's eyes watered as she hurried to open the door and grab a pair of pot holders to fan the fire alarm. So much for her perfect dinner. Her tartlets were hidden in the back of the deep-freeze as possible evidence for Mr. Woodruff's death, the roast pork was a piece of charcoal, and her almond and orange cake for the baked Alaska flambé sat dried out on the countertop. All her grand visions of wowing the guests vanished.

The buzzing alarm finally stopped.

Nathan stepped inside the kitchen doorway and coughed. "What happened? I was out at the barn, telling Oscar about Charles and warning dinner would be late."

Neither Oscar Philips, Nathan's professional guide, nor any of the guests would be eating dinner soon. With a pot holder in each hand, Pricilla pulled out the pan holding the charred remains. "My roast pork. Need I say more?"

"With all that's happened tonight, I'm not at all surprised no one remembered to turn the oven off." Nathan crossed the room and took the heavy dish out of her hands.

"Not only that, the dial is set as high as it can go. I must have turned it up instead of off. Strange—I never do that sort of thing. No wonder it set off the smoke alarm." Pricilla fanned herself with the pot holders as Max took the pan from Nathan then went to throw it into the garbage bin outside. "At least the smoke's clearing. What a complete waste."

"Don't worry about it, Mom."

The roast wasn't all she was worried about.

"What about the guests? Everyone must be starving." She started to rummage through the refrigerator, trying to come up with a spur-of-the-moment meal for ten people. "There are some cold cuts for sandwiches and—"

"I meant it when I said don't worry about it, Mom. Simon Wheeler and his buddies left for town a few minutes ago. I gave them a voucher to the Rendezvous Bar and Grill, so they'll be fine."

"What about Trisha and Max and—"

"Trisha is upstairs with Claire, and I've already

told her I'd bring her something to eat after everything settles down. She wanted to stay with Claire until she fell asleep." Nathan wrapped his arm around his mother and pulled her close. "I'll make sandwiches for Trisha and me. I'll make you one as well if you promise to forget about the kitchen and then go get some sleep. It's been a long day for all of us."

Pricilla shook her head. The thought of food made her stomach revolt. "I couldn't eat a bite, but I do need to salvage what I can from tonight's fiasco."

Max returned with the now-empty baking dish and started rinsing it in the sink. "I heard what Nathan said, and he's right, Pricilla. We all need a good night's sleep. Especially you."

"Just a few more minutes." She grabbed a food storage bag out of a drawer and started putting the rolls in it. Reheated, she could serve them for lunch tomorrow with the beef stew she planned to fix. That is if anyone would dare try her cooking.

Misty, the housekeeper, entered the kitchen out of breath. "Sorry I've not been here to help clean up, Mrs. Crumb. Trisha asked me to get some things out of Mrs. Woodruff's car for her. The woman's quite distraught. We heard the smoke alarm go off, but by the time we convinced Claire to hurry outside in case it was a real fire, the alarm had stopped. Is everything all right?"

"I apparently never turned off the oven," Pricilla said, trying to take comfort in the fact that it was only her roast pork and not the lodge that had been demolished. "If you're hungry—"

"Oh no, ma'am." The young woman pressed her hands against her stomach. "I could never eat after seeing Mr. Woodruff hunched over like a rag doll in that chair. I've never seen a dead person in real life before, you know, and his skin was so pale and—"

"We all saw him as well." Pricilla shuddered at the image, not wanting to be reminded of the details. "It's been a disturbing evening for all of us."

"I feel sorry for his wife," Misty said, "though if you ask me, Mr. Woodruff wasn't the nicest man in the world."

"Why do you say that?" Pricilla asked, busying herself with the last of the cleanup while the men started making the sandwiches.

Misty's gaze dropped, and Pricilla wondered if the housekeeper knew something the rest of them didn't. Nathan had told her Misty had worked for him about eight years, so Pricilla was quite certain that the twenty-something-year-old knew a lot about the guests. Especially guests who returned every year.

Misty pulled on a strand of her long blond hair and began twirling it with her fingers. "Didn't you hear them fighting this afternoon?"

"All couples fight from time to time." While Pricilla would never admit to intentionally listening to their conversation, she was certain that everyone in the lodge had witnessed Mr. and Mrs. Woodruff's raised voices as they went up to their room. She hadn't made out everything they were saying, but the tone of their conversation was evident. Charles had been furious about something. "Conflict and problem solving are a part of being married."

"That might be true, but engaging in an argument with Charles Woodruff has never been difficult." Nathan opened the almost empty jar of mayonnaise and began spreading some on the bread he'd laid out. "Even I had a heated discussion with the man on his arrival. He never was very amiable."

Misty shuddered. "If you don't mind, I'd like to go home now. My heart just won't stop pounding."

"Of course you can," Pricilla assured her. "It's been a rough evening on all of us."

Nathan held up the jar as Misty headed out the back door toward her cabin. "Is there any more?"

"Top shelf in the pantry." There was something else bothering her, and Pricilla wondered if she should say what was on her mind. "You know, Misty does have an interesting point."

"What's that?" Max asked.

"From what I've noticed, Charles wasn't exactly the most well-liked person. What if it wasn't my tartlets that poisoned him, and he didn't have a heart attack—"

"Don't even go there, Mom." Nathan frowned as he grabbed the new jar off the shelf.

"He's right, Pricilla." Max turned around and faced her. "I don't think we have anything to worry about this being anything other than a heart attack."

The men had to be right. She'd never sleep tonight

if she let her mind wander in the direction of murder—because that would mean there was a murderer on the loose.

Still, if there was a hint of foul play, she wasn't certain a small town like Rendezvous would have the necessary resources to deal with a situation like this. How long might it take before Detective Carter managed to obtain the results? She wasn't convinced of the man's competence. It wasn't as if they had a team of crime scene investigators on hand like they did on television. They'd have to call for help and there was no telling how long that might take. Pricilla remembered Nathan saying that the last unexplained death that had occurred in this town was ten years ago. The town librarian had been found dead at the bank of Lake Paytah wearing a purple scuba-diving suit. To this day the crime hadn't been solved.

Pricilla grabbed some foil from the drawer to begin wrapping up the cake. She might have watched too many reruns of *Murder, She Wrote* and *Father Dowling*, but all the same, she couldn't shake the eerie feeling she had about the whole situation. A dead man wasn't exactly something she had to deal with every day.

"Has anyone called a doctor to come check on Claire?" Pricilla asked, still trying to get the image of Charles Woodruff's body out of her mind.

"I did. Doc Freeman's up the mountain, delivering a baby." Nathan dumped a handful of potato chips beside the sandwich on his plate and then did the same for

Trisha's plate. "He said he wouldn't be available until the morning, and he couldn't do much anyway. Said to give Claire an over-the-counter sleeping pill if she wanted it, and to call him tomorrow. I offered her one and she took it, so hopefully she'll get some rest tonight."

She watched Max pull a cold drink out of the refrigerator and pop the tab open, but despite his presence, the situation still left her feeling vulnerable. The sheriff was out of town and had left an inexperienced detective in charge. Now the town's one doctor was unavailable.

"What does one do around here if there's a real crisis?"

Nathan laughed, breaking some of the tension in the room. "We've always done pretty well at avoiding one until tonight."

At least if she was in the middle of a crisis, which was the way she classified this situation, Nathan and Max were the two men she'd want to have by her side. A wave of exhaustion struck her, and she grabbed the edge of the counter to steady herself. Glancing around the kitchen, she decided it was clean enough for now. Any more excitement tonight and they'd be calling Dr. Freeman for her.

"I think I'll take a cup of herbal tea now after all and then go on to bed. I was planning to check on Claire myself, but it seems as if Trisha has everything under control." Pricilla set a mug of lukewarm water in the microwave to reheat it and pressed START. "I remember the night Marty died. The reality of what had happened didn't hit me until the next day. Tomorrow will be difficult."

"You're right," Nathan said. "Claire and Charles didn't have any close family. I've told her she's welcome to stay a few extra days if she needs to."

"What about tomorrow's hunting trip?" Max asked before chomping into his sandwich.

Nathan wiped a crumb off his chin. "The detective said we can go ahead with the hunting trip as planned. I know it will be early, Mom, but—"

The microwave dinged and Pricilla pulled the mug out. "I'll have a hot breakfast on the table by six."

⟶

Max watched Pricilla walk out of the kitchen. No matter what the cause of Charles Woodruff's death, the evening had been quite disturbing to all of them. Pricilla's believing it was her fault only compounded the matter. And as unrealistic as it was, thoughts of a real murderer made his skin crawl.

Needing something stronger than a cup of tea, Max poured himself a mug of leftover coffee from the coffee maker to go with his sandwich then offered Nathan some of the hazelnut-flavored brew.

"Guess I need something to wash this food down with. Can't help but wish I was eating some of my mom's roast and hot yeast rolls right now, though."

"I'm with you on that one." Max chuckled.

Nathan rested his hands against the counter. "I'm worried about her."

Max took a sip of the coffee and decided to nuke it in the microwave. "Pricilla's a strong woman. Imaginative, granted, but very strong. She'll be fine."

"I know. It's just that she worked so hard on tonight's dinner, and now to have her think that she murdered someone with her tartlets. . ."

Max tried not to laugh.

While the very idea of Pricilla's tartlets being the cause of Mr. Woodruff's demise was absurd, he knew it made perfect sense to her. Maybe that was one reason he enjoyed being around her so much. He never knew what to expect from her. She had that offbeat, quirky sense of humor that always made him smile. And the older he got, the more important laughter became.

"You know I would never tease her. It's actually much more than that." What could he say? That he had another reason for coming? Could he tell Nathan he'd hoped that he and Pricilla might discover something deeper than friendship?

"You're in love with her, aren't you?"

Max caught Nathan's gaze and swallowed hard, amazed at Nathan's perception.

"*Love* is a pretty strong word." He wanted a change in his relationship with Pricilla, but was he ready to say he loved her? He pulled the sugar bowl out of the cupboard and added two spoonfuls to his coffee before heating both mugs in the microwave. "She makes me smile and feel young. I can talk to her about anything, from politics, to spiritual issues, to the latest reality show."

"You're going to have your hands full."

This time Max laughed out loud. "Trust me. I've known your mother long enough to know both her weaknesses and her strengths. I spent over half my life in the military, learning how to negotiate, talk peace, and delegate responsibilities. I think I'm prepared to handle just about anything."

"Your daughter's a lot like you, you know." Nathan took a sip of his coffee. "I'm impressed with the way she's jumped in and helped to smooth out a difficult situation with my guests."

Max didn't miss the smile that reached all the way to the corners of Nathan's eyes. For once it seemed that Pricilla might have been right on track when she decided to put her matchmaking skills to the test. The spark between Nathan and Trisha seemed to have been lit from the moment they met.

"Trisha's always had her head on straight. I don't know what I'd do without her."

Nathan set his mug down on the counter with a thud. "My mother's trying to set me up with her, isn't she?"

"And it's taken you this long to figure that out?"

Nathan shook his head. "So you're in on it?"

"I'll never admit to that."

Now it was Nathan's turn to laugh. "It doesn't matter, I suppose. I really like Trisha. She might not be the outdoor type, but I've already discovered that we have plenty of things in common. Books, science-fiction movies, country music. . ."

"You still sound a bit hesitant."

"Let's just say I've never made time for having a relationship. The lodge is my life, and I love what I do."

"And now?"

Nathan shrugged a shoulder. "I don't know, except I'm glad I'm working at the lodge this week instead of hunting."

"Just promise me that you won't tell your mother, or Trisha, we had this discussion."

"Don't worry," Nathan said. "This time I have as much at stake as you do."

Normally, the scent of frying bacon and a glass of orange juice was enough to get Pricilla going. This morning she'd gone for a cup of coffee, something she normally avoided because of the caffeine, but even her second cup wasn't doing the trick.

"Good morning." Max's smile was far too cheery. "Did you sleep well?"

"Barely a wink." She wouldn't tell him that when she *had* slept, her sleep had been full of troubled dreams.

"You should have taken one of your sleeping pills."

"I would have, but I needed to get up early, and I didn't want to take the chance of being drowsy." She yawned. "Now I'm regretting it."

"What can I do to help?" He tugged on the bottom of his hunter green jacket.

Pricilla glanced at him. She'd always thought Max handsome, with his bright blue eyes and dark brows. His hair had grayed over the years, but he still was as handsome as he'd been when they'd first met, with his broad shoulders and military physique. . . .

She shook her head and tried to control her rambling thoughts. "The sausage needs to be turned. I just need to finish cooking the rest of the pancake batter, and we can eat."

Max grabbed a pair of tongs and begun turning the thick slices of sausage. "Would it help if I stayed behind? I wouldn't mind a bit."

"Yes, you would." She ignored the strong urge to accept his offer. "You'd be holed up with a bunch of women for a week and be miserable."

"I'd get your cooking every night."

Pricilla could feel the heat rising in her cheeks and tried to decipher the look in Max's eyes. "If you bring some game back, I promise to make you a full course meal fit for a king when you return."

"With one of your lemon crumb cakes for dessert?"

"Of course." She busied herself with flipping the

pancakes. "I'll watch the sausage, if you wouldn't mind ringing the bell on the front porch and calling everyone in to eat?"

As Pricilla watched Max leave the room, she tried to swallow the disappointment she felt, knowing he wouldn't be here for most of the week. The feeling surprised her. She'd always enjoyed Max's company, but they rarely had the opportunity to spend time with each other. Phone calls and letters had been their way of communicating. Why then would she feel any different this morning? More than likely it was simply because she was sleep deprived. She never functioned well this early in the morning.

A loud *crash* resounded from outside. Then someone yelled.

Max?

It was a sudden déjà vu from the night before. Pricilla's heart shuddered, as she jerked the sausage off the stove and dashed toward the front door. One dead body had been enough to leave her on edge. A second incident might just be enough to push her tumbling over the side.

4

Pricilla stumbled out the front door and found Max lying face down at the bottom of the stairs on a patch of grass. She ran across the porch, ignoring the achy throb in her left hip that told her to slow down. If anything happened to Max she'd never forgive herself for inviting him here.

Oh Lord, please let him be all right—

Her mind tried to push away the insane image that they had a murderer on the loose, but after a restless night with little sleep, she wasn't thinking clearly. Bizarre dreams of Charles Woodruff sitting in front of the fireplace, eating piles and piles of her tartlets before keeling over didn't help either. No, she had to believe Max and Nathan's strong admonitions that she had nothing to do with Charles's untimely demise. That was difficult to achieve. Surely it wasn't simply a coincidence that first Charles had collapsed and now Max?

She knelt beside him and reached for his wrist to check his pulse. Nothing. She tried his neck, but she still couldn't feel anything. No pulse meant—

Max groaned. He slowly rolled into a sitting position, and Pricilla let out a sigh of relief. He might be injured, but at least he wasn't dead. And there was no sign of blood.

Her heart pounded. "What in the world happened?"

"It's my ankle. I tripped."

She grabbed his arm to help him up, but he stopped her. He may not have lost his life to some crazed lunatic, but he obviously felt he'd lost a measure of his dignity. Ignoring her offer to help, he struggled to stand.

After a minute of trying, he sat back down on the grass and squeezed his eyes shut. "I think I'm going to need your help after all."

Somehow, between the two of them, they managed to get him onto the porch steps where he could sit and elevate his leg.

Once he was settled, Pricilla glanced out across the front grounds. The thick vegetation provided plenty of places where a perpetrator could disappear. The same thing was true along the front of the lodge. Thick shrubs lined the porch. If someone had pushed Max, there were plenty of places to hide, but why? A connection to Charles didn't make sense. The two men didn't even know each other.

Unless the lodge was the connection. Was there someone with a vendetta against Nathan? Perhaps a disgruntled employee who wanted retribution? She'd have to ask her son.

She sat beside Max and rested his foot in her lap despite his protests. "I need to know if someone pushed you."

"If someone pushed me?" His eyes widened as she worked to untie the laces, and she wasn't sure if it was from the pain or her question.

"This isn't an episode of *Murder, She Wrote*, Pricilla. I tripped."

"All right. But I couldn't help wondering. I just thought with Charles—" Pricilla closed her mouth, feeling quite foolish. Max obviously wasn't connecting the two incidents. Nathan wouldn't either.

She untied the shoe and gently pulled it from his foot.

"Ouch."

"I'm sorry, but your shoe has to come off. Your ankle is already beginning to swell."

"I'm the one who should be sorry." Max shook his head. "I shouldn't have snapped at you. This certainly isn't your fault. I've either broken it, or done a fine job of twisting it. So much for my plans for the week."

She could read the disappointment in his face. "Your hunting trip—"

"I know. Of all the ridiculous things to have happen." Pricilla managed to keep her mouth shut this time and let him rant. "For thirty-five years I trained soldiers, led reconnaissance missions, and tracked down bad guys, with nothing more than a few scratches, and now I've tripped down a stupid staircase and broken something."

She started to take off his thick black sock then stopped. What did one do with a broken bone?

Pricilla shuddered at the thought. She'd mastered the art of cooking, but broken bones, blood. . .dead bodies. . .these were things she couldn't handle. She tried to focus on the issue at hand. They should immobilize the ankle, and they needed ice. She knew that. But a doctor would need to look at it.

She put down his foot gently on the step then started up the stairs. "I'll get the keys to the car and some ice from the kitchen. I'm going to take you into town to the clinic."

There were no arguments from Max as Pricilla hurried into the house. The smell of burnt pancakes wafted from the kitchen. Great. Not only had she managed to totally destroy last night's dinner, now she was doing a good job of ruining today's breakfast. Thankfully she'd thought to pull the sausage off the burner, but the last batch of pancakes hadn't fared so well. She turned off the electric skillet then dumped the blackened pancakes down the garbage disposal.

Pricilla let out a sigh. At least this morning the damage was far less, though if she wasn't careful, her entire reputation as a good cook was going to be ruined even if her tartlets weren't the cause of Charles Woodruff's death.

She put the sausage in a warming dish and shoved it into the oven. Where was Misty when she needed her?

As if she'd heard the question, Misty appeared in the back doorway.

"You're late," Pricilla said, before the young woman had a chance to speak.

"I'm sorry, Mrs. Crumb. The children were difficult this morning and—"

"It's all right." She waved her hand. She knew she

shouldn't take out her frustration on Misty.

Pricilla grabbed the keys from the kitchen drawer and a bag of frozen peas, all the while giving Misty instructions as to how she wanted breakfast served. By the time she made it back to the porch, Trisha was kneeling beside her father.

The young woman looked up at Pricilla. "I told Dad if he really wanted to stay behind with the women this week, he could have come up with an easier solution."

"You're a bunch of laughs, Trisha," Max said with a frown. "Help me to the car, will you?"

Five minutes later, Pricilla was driving Max into town. Trisha stayed behind to keep an eye on Claire. Max, stretched out in the back sat seat with the bag of frozen peas resting on his ankle, was quiet as Pricilla followed the dirt road that would soon be covered in snow.

While she was relieved that Max's fall seemed to be a completely isolated incident, it didn't change the fact that she could still be responsible for Charles's death. She wondered how long they sent one to prison for involuntary manslaughter.

She also wondered if any of the guests had decided to show up and eat the breakfast Misty was now serving. Already, she could envision poisonous mushrooms in her fluffy omelets and botulism in the homemade sausage.

"You're still blaming yourself, aren't you?"

Pricilla coughed, wondering how Max always seemed to read her mind. "I can't help it. I've got this feeling that something's wrong, and if it wasn't my tartlets. . ." She couldn't let herself think too long on the alternative. "Do you really think Charles died of natural causes?"

"Of course." Was that hesitation in his voice, or was she imagining that as well? "Just because someone dies unexpectedly doesn't mean foul play is involved. And it certainly doesn't mean your tartlets were involved."

"We'll see." She hoped they would have some answers from the toxicology report soon. Waiting was torture.

Max reached up and patted her arm. "Didn't Jesus say not to worry about your life?"

"He said don't worry about tomorrow, but He also said each day has enough trouble of its own. Seems like during these past twenty-four hours we've had enough trouble for at least a month or two."

His deep laughed stopped abruptly as the right tire hit a pothole.

"Sorry. Is the pain bad?"

"Minimal."

She didn't believe him at all, but Max was a soldier, and his type didn't give in to pain.

"You have to admit it's odd." Pricilla hoped that talking would distract him from the pain. "First Charles keels over and dies unexpectedly and then you fall down the stairs."

"It's a coincidence, Pricilla. Nothing more. Let the detective handle things and forget it."

She didn't miss the sharp look he shot her. It was time to drop the subject.

~

Doc Freeman was back in the clinic and his diagnosis was better than Max expected. But as they left two hours later to head back to the lodge, he was still furious at himself. Even a sprained ankle, the doctor had informed him, could take up to six weeks to fully mend. Possibly longer at his age.

Despite his frustration, he was proud of Pricilla. While they had waited in the cramped lobby, not once had she brought up the subject of Charles's death. Not that he wasn't convinced that her mind was still fully engaged and trying to figure out what had happened, but at least she'd kept any comments to herself. Instead, they passed the time talking about their last vacations, what was happening in their churches, and their children.

He carefully turned his leg to try and relieve some of the pressure. "I appreciate your taking me to the doctor this morning."

"At least it's not broken."

He might be furious at himself for making such a stupid error, but there was a bright side to it all. "There is something good that will come out of this."

"And what would that be?"

"When's the last time we were able to spend an entire week together?"

Her brow wrinkled slightly. "I don't believe we ever have."

Max nodded. "Exactly."

She frowned, but he didn't miss the twinkle in her eyes. "You just want to keep your eye on me, don't you?"

"Perhaps partly, but I am looking forward to some of your cooking."

Hearing her laughter reminded him of why he'd always been drawn to Pricilla and what a kind-hearted woman she was.

"If I can manage to get through a meal without burning something."

"I'm sure the rest of the week will be different."

Max leaned back in the seat and smiled, thankful that the painkillers the doctor had given him were finally starting to kick in. While Pricilla might be nosy and even meddlesome at times, he also knew that she was also forgiving, loving, and would do anything for anyone. He couldn't help but love her. . . .

Love her?

The thought took him by surprise. Had Nathan been right? He shifted again and looked at her out of the corner of his eye. He fought the urge to reach out and run his fingers down the side of her cheek. In the week ahead of him, he was going to have nothing to do but spend time with Pricilla. She might be full of matchmaking schemes for their children, but he wondered if she ever thought about herself. Maybe she wasn't the only one who needed a matchmaking plan to put into action.

"I do have one question for you," Pricilla said as they turned off the main road and onto the dirt lane that would take them back to the lodge.

He temporarily set aside his thoughts of courting. "What's that?"

"You don't have to go down the stairs on the front porch to ring the bell. How did you end up falling down the stairs?"

Max knew he had to choose his words carefully. He wasn't sure he should tell her. All she needed was more fuel for her imagination. Something that was already close to exploding into an inferno. "There is one other thing that happened this morning that I didn't tell you."

"What are you talking about?"

"It's probably nothing."

"Max. . ."

"I was about to ring the bell, when I noticed something moving along the side of the barn. At first I thought it might be an animal, but as I moved toward the stairs, it was obvious that it wasn't."

"It was a person?"

"Yes, but I'm not sure who." He shrugged. "More than likely it was just Oscar getting things together for the hunting trip."

Pricilla slowed the car as they drove through the main gate. "Seems strange that someone would be lurking around the barn. Even Oscar would use the main entrance."

"It was nothing, Pricilla. I shouldn't have told you."

He leaned down to the floorboard to pick up his sack of prescriptions and winced at the movement. The doctor had told him to take the medicine and rest for a couple of days, a plan he fully intended to follow.

Pricilla put her foot on the brake and brought the car to a jolting stop. "Maybe you should tell the sheriff then."

"What?" Max winced at the pain and braced himself with his hands against the dashboard.

"Look." She sucked in a deep breath.

Max's jaw line tensed. Any plans for romance might very well have to be laid to rest. The lodge was surrounded by sheriff's vehicles.

5

Pricilla parked the car in front of the lodge, but didn't make any move to get out. A wave of dizziness swept over her. She prayed she wouldn't pass out and make a total fool out of herself, but three vehicles clearly meant that Charles's death had not occurred under ordinary circumstances. Which left two alternatives in her mind. Either Charles had died from food poisoning. . .or there was a murderer involved. Both options left her wanting to jump on the next airplane back to Seattle.

"Aren't you getting out of the car?" Max asked.

"If I have a choice? No." Pricilla dangled the keys in front of her. "There are two options we're looking at here, Max, and I don't like either one. The authorities are here, which means that either my tartlets were involved with Charles's death, or someone murdered him."

He shook his head. "We don't know anything yet."

"Then why are there three, count them, three of the sheriff's cars outside the lodge the morning after one of the guests keels over with no warning?"

Max drummed his fingers on the armrest. "There could be a number of other explanations."

"Give me one." She waited for him to respond. He didn't, making an even stronger argument for her deductions. "You see. You can't think of any other options either."

He shot her a wry smile. "Maybe something happened while we were gone this morning."

She didn't like this explanation any better. "Like what? Guest number two collapses after eating my homemade sausage—"

Max reached out to squeeze her hand. "I told you to stop blaming yourself. Until they find absolute proof that you were involved, you need to stop worrying."

"Stop worrying!" She thumped the steering wheel in frustration. "That, my dear, is certainly easier said than done."

Pricilla stepped out of the car then yanked the rented crutches out of the back. Max was not helping. Something had obviously happened, and she had an unsettled feeling in her stomach that said it wasn't good.

Max hobbled beside her down the graveled driveway until they reached the porch, where she managed to help him up the stairs and into the lodge.

"Mom. I'm glad you're back." Nathan's boots thudded against the smooth tiled entryway as he met them inside the lodge. "I'm sorry about the injury, Max. Are you all right?"

Max paused in the doorway. "Thankfully, the doctor says it's just sprained."

Pricilla touched the sleeve of her son's sweater. "Please tell us what's going on here. Considering the size of Rendezvous, it looks as if the cavalry has arrived."

From the troubled expression on Nathan's face, she sensed he was worried. "I guess you could say that. Detective Carter decided to show up with reinforcements."

"I can see that, but why?" Pricilla followed the men down the short hallway toward the living room.

"Apparently there have been some unsettling findings regarding Mr. Woodruff's death, though I can't get anything out of the detective. We're all supposed to meet in the living room."

"Wonderful. He's summoning us like a group of suspects."

"Mrs. Crumb." Detective Carter met them in the hallway. His voice was friendly, but the sentiment was short lived. "We've been awaiting your arrival. I'm sure you're anxious to hear our preliminary findings."

"I'm surprised you have something to report so soon." Pricilla looked the detective in the eye and frowned. The man was obviously out to prove something, though what, she wasn't sure.

"It's my job to bring about justice as quickly as possible."

Pricilla entered the living room behind Max then took a seat between him and Nathan on the soft leather couch. While she'd always enjoyed the open and rustic décor of the room, with its wooden ceiling beams and beautiful pine furniture, today it seemed as cold as the expressions on the guests' faces. Claire's pale appearance emphasized the fact that she would rather be anywhere else. And the men, no doubt, would rather be heading for the mountains and their chance for another trophy.

Simon seemed the most sullen of the three friends. He looked liked he hadn't shaved in several days and the old baseball cap shoved backward on his head managed only to partly cover his unruly mop of dark, curly hair. Anthony perched on the edge of his chair next to Simon, wearing a red T-shirt and flannel shirt that both looked as if they'd been slept in. He eyed the doorway as if he were contemplating a quick getaway. Michael was the only one who apparently hadn't broken away from the formalities of the business world's dress code. Clean shaven, with only a goatee marking his chocolate-colored skin, and decked out in a fleece vest and camouflage pants, he could have posed as a model for any number of hunting magazines.

Pricilla turned her attention to Detective Carter, who stood with his back to the fireplace as he pulled out his little notebook from the back pocket of his pants.

The detective cleared his throat as Oscar and Misty slipped into the room then flipped open his spiraled notepad. "I'm sure you're wondering why I've called you all together this morning. What I had hoped would be a simple case of a heart attack has unfortunately turned into something much more serious."

Pricilla's eyes widened. She didn't like where this was going. Had Charles Woodruff died of food poisoning, or something more sinister?

"Normally an autopsy takes at least twenty-four hours," the detective continued, "but thankfully things fell into place a bit quicker on this case. At first it appeared that there was no real reason to even have an autopsy performed, but during my investigation yesterday, several things stood out that bothered me."

Pricilla saw Claire catch her breath. Yesterday, the detective had assured them that there was no reason to suspect foul play. What had happened between then and now to bring such a turnaround in his position? Certainly Sheriff Tucker wouldn't be handling things this way if he were here. Having them assemble in the living room like a bunch of suspects and Detective Carter carrying on as if he were a Sherlock Holmes wannabe was nothing more than a theatrical stunt.

The detective took a step away from the fireplace and tapped his pen against the notebook. "The first thing that struck me was Mrs. Woodruff's insistence that her husband was in perfect health. To any officer of the law, this raises a question in his mind, when one then expires so unexpectedly. Secondly, there was Mrs. Crumb's assertion that her tartlets had been the cause of his untimely death."

Max reached out and took Pricilla's hand. Despite the comfort it gave her, this time she avoided his gaze. No one had to remind her that, even after living sixty plus years, she still hadn't mastered the art of patience. Oh no. She had to be the one to throw herself in front of the detective, practically begging for him to haul her off to jail for murder. Maybe someday she'd learn to keep her mouth shut, but that wasn't going to help her today.

The detective turned toward her, and she heard the clank of his metal handcuffs. "Both instances sent up red flags in my mind. While it will still be some time before the toxicology report is in as well as the official autopsy report from the coroner, the preliminary results are startling."

Pricilla leaned forward in her chair and forced herself not to jump up and grab the detective's notebook from him so she could get to the bottom line.

But the man wasn't finished. "Before I accepted the position of detective to the fine town of Rendezvous and the surrounding areas, I was privileged to participate in a number of forensic classes in Denver. The presence of poisons in a deceased body can be detected in outward signs. For instance, cyanide has a bitter almond odor detectable on the body. Be that as it may, few people are able to detect the smell of hydrogen cyanide. Fortunately, I happen to be one who can."

The detective addressed them as if they were a group of college freshman who didn't know anything. "Cyanide also turns the blood a bright cherry red. And this precisely is what was discovered in Mr. Woodruff's body. While the findings are preliminary, of course, I have enough to warrant an investigation."

Pricilla had to force herself to take a breath. Cyanide? Surely the detective wasn't accusing her of purposely poisoning Charles?

"Mrs. Crumb"—the detective shortened the gap between them—"you can rest assured that while we will have to test your tartlets, at the present moment, we don't suspect that they had anything to do with Mr. Woodruff's death, though I can't tell you the specifics as to why at the moment."

Pricilla let out an audible sigh of relief.

"But we do, in fact, have reason to believe that Charles Woodruff might have been murdered." He tapped the notebook against the palm of his hand. "I must ask you to stay away from the crime scene."

Max raised his hand. "May I ask a question?"

The detective shoved his notebook back into his pocket. "Before I try to answer any questions, there is one more thing that must be made clear. No one will be allowed to leave the area until further notice. That will be all for now."

A number of audible moans filled the room at the untimely announcement. Several of them gathered around the detective, firing off questions to the balding man, while others slipped out of the room. Claire sat riveted in her seat.

Pricilla slipped into the chair beside her. "I'm sorry about all of this. I know it must be frightening. If there's anything I can do—"

The woman stared at the braided rug at her feet. "The detective told me ahead of time what he was going to announce. I just didn't expect it to be such a shock, hearing it the second time."

Pricilla tugged on the edge of her jacket, searching for words of encouragement. "Do you have family? Anyone close who could come be with you during this difficult time?"

Claire hiccupped and wiped a tear from her cheek with the back of her hand. "Charles and I had plenty of social friends, but no true friends."

"What about funeral arrangements?" Pricilla pulled out a clean tissue from her pocket and handed it to Claire.

The woman nodded her thanks then blew her nose. "Once the state is finished with his body, I'm having it sent to California where I'll bury him. . .and then have a small memorial service that likely no one will attend."

"I'm sure that's not true."

"You didn't know my husband." For the first time, Claire turned and looked at her. "There was a charismatic side of him that people liked, so much so that he was planning to go into politics. But he was so afraid people would find out that he wasn't perfect. We had to have the right house, the right car, the right vacation. Eventually he cut us off from all our friends, family. . . ."

"Do you have a church family?"

Claire let out a low chuckle. "Charles wasn't one for religion, and I pretty much gave up what little faith I had when I met him."

The thought broke Pricilla's heart. She wasn't

sure she would have made it after Marty died, if it hadn't been for her relationship with God along with the support of her friends at church, and her family. Unfortunately, she'd met far too many people like Claire. Women, especially, who had left their faith because of a boyfriend or husband. It might take time for Claire to realize how important it was, but there was always hope.

"It's never too late to—"

"It's too late for Charles." Claire stood up and wrapped her sweater around her. "I'm sorry, Mrs. Crumb. I appreciate your kindness, but all of this has been such a shock. I think I will go upstairs and rest. They've moved me to another room, thankfully, and your son is being kind enough to allow me to stay. I just wished things would have turned out different."

"We all do, Mrs. Woodruff."

Pricilla got up slowly from the cushioned chair and felt quite her age at the moment. There was no doubt about another thing as well. Her guest list had just turned into a suspect list—for murder.

———

"We've got to think of something better than this." Pricilla looked over the list before handing it on to Trisha. "Until our detective finishes his investigation, I can hardly see a man like Simon Wheeler playing a competitive game of croquet."

Trisha threw the notebook down onto Nathan's desk and nodded her head. "You do have a point, but we've got to decide on something."

Nathan raked his fingers through his hair. "That's easy to say, but if I wanted to be an entertainment director, I'd have applied for a position on the Love Boat."

Pricilla stifled a laugh, but she had to agree. Hunting, fishing, and camping trips were what had made the lodge a success. Canceling the hunting trip, and the men's chance for another set of antlers for their trophy walls, was like a death sentence. Max, Nathan, Trisha, and Pricilla had worked for an hour to come up with ideas to keep their guests happy until the detective let them go. Carter had insisted that the hunting trip be postponed. The whole procedure was becoming ridiculous, and it was evident that Detective Carter was determined to stay in control.

Pricilla tried to come up with something unique. Hunting. . .guns—that was it!

She sat forward on the edge of her chair. "What do these men like to do?"

Nathan shot her a puzzled look. "They love to hunt."

"Exactly. Which means these men love guns. They love to shoot and compete. So what about setting up some sort of competition for them?"

"Skeet shooting and clay targets." Max threw out.

"And we could bring in some of the locals?" Trisha grabbed the notepad and started jotting down ideas.

Nathan tapped the edge of his desk and smiled. "That's the best idea we've heard so far. As long as the competition is kept a safe distance from the house, we could invite the community and not worry about the crime scene. We could even throw in a few prizes. We need to start calling everyone we know in town—"

The phone rang. Nathan answered it and then frowned.

"No, I can only verify what the police report says. We have no further information for you," he said firmly. "No, the victim's wife isn't making any statements, and neither is the lodge. No. . .no. . .I'm sorry, but this is private property and we'd rather not have any photographers disrupting our other guests' visits. Sorry I can't help you further. Thank you. Good-bye." Nathan was shaking his head as he hung up.

"Great. The *Rendezvous Sentinel* got word of Charles and now they're going to put the story on tomorrow's front page. They don't know yet that it may be murder, but how many reservations will it kill? We've already had two cancellations just today. I'll go out of business if this keeps up."

"The town paper is small potatoes, but it can tip off bigger media," said Trisha. "We can post an announcement on the lodge's Web site. But I think you need to get on the phone and call the sheriff and the editor and the chamber of commerce and the state tourism council and your pastor and your attorney and anyone else you can think of." She took a breath. "We can't just roll over dead."

She stood up and strode toward the picture window that looked out over the snow-dusted mountain.

"You're right. I called and left Sheriff Tucker a message right after the detective made his announcement and called off the hunting trip. I'm waiting to hear back from him."

There was a knock on the door and Pricilla glanced up to see Simon Wheeler in the doorway.

"Mr. Wheeler, can I help you?" Nathan stood and walked to the door.

The frown on the guest's face made it clear that his reason for stopping by Nathan's office was not for a pleasant chat. "I came here to go hunting and paid a lot of money to get what I have always considered to be the best hunting experience around."

"I'm glad you think that way, Mr.—"

"I'm not finished. What has happened here is unacceptable—"

"Mr. Wheeler"—Nathan held up his hand—"you have to understand that while the lodge plans to do all it can to compensate for your week, there are simply things that are out of our control. If you have a problem with the way things stand then you'll need to take your complaints to the detective."

"I've done that, but that man won't change his mind." Simon stepped forward and slapped his hands against the top of the desk. "What do you suppose we do in the meantime? I didn't come here to sit around reading and drinking hot chocolate all day."

"I'm sure you didn't." Nathan held up his notepad. "The four of us have been putting together a program of activities that should keep everyone busy until the detective gives the word that we all can leave."

Mr. Wheeler looked skeptical. "Activities? This isn't a junior high camp."

"Of course not." Trisha stepped forward, giving the man his best smile. "We are thinking more in line of things like a skeet-shooting competition with prizes."

The man rubbed his goatee.

"And plenty of food," Pricilla added.

Trisha nodded. "Give the detective another day or two and in the meantime, I'm sure that Nathan will do all he can to get permission to get the hunting trip back on the calendar."

Pricilla smiled with relief as Simon finally left the room. Trisha was not only beautiful, but an intelligent negotiator as well. The girl was the perfect complement for Nathan. Listening to the young woman's well-spoken argument had brought a ray of hope. And, despite Charles's untimely demise, Cupid's arrow might hit Nathan and Trisha after all.

Detective Carter appeared in the doorway. "Sorry to bother you, Nathan. I'm on my way back to the station and wondered if you wouldn't mind coming with me? I just have a few questions I'd like to ask you."

Any relief Pricilla had felt vanished. "I think it's time you called your lawyer, Nathan."

Nathan stood up and grabbed his coat off the rack. "I don't have anything to hide, Mom. Besides, the sooner we find the truth, the sooner we can get our lives back to normal."

6

For the first time in twenty-odd years, Pricilla decided to forgo the planned home-cooked spread and decided to serve cold cuts for lunch. While such fare might be common for half the population's noon meal, she'd always insisted on something heartier, and over the years had pledged to avoid serving cold sandwiches to company. In spite of all her good intentions, though, today it couldn't be avoided. She could only hope that the guests wouldn't complain about her lowered standards if she did it just this once.

She stood with the refrigerator door open, debating if roast beef, ham, and turkey would be enough of a selection. Her mother had taught her the importance of making meal time a priority family time. Meals in her house growing up had always been a place where family members came together to share what had happened during the day. Pricilla had, in turn, carried on the same tradition in her own family, and while she couldn't implement such traditions on the guests, it was her responsibility to insure they had the most pleasant dining experience possible. Withdrawing a bag of carrots from the refrigerator to add to her pile of lunch ingredients, she tried to ignore the strong feelings of guilt that began to surface at her compromise.

Guilt—and anger.

She pulled a knife out of the butcher block and started slicing the carrots into thin julienne strips. Taking Max to the doctor might have given her less time to prepare lunch, but the morning's time crunch wasn't what had her upset. What worried her was Nathan. She slammed the knife against the wooden cutting board. Detective Carter had no right to haul her son down to the station. She'd watched enough episodes of *Father Dowling* to know what that implied. A friendly invitation to the sheriff's office meant nothing other than her son was now considered a suspect in a murder investigation. A thought that was absolutely ridiculous.

Pricilla dropped the knife and gnawed on her lower lip. With the detective's decision to involve her son, the stakes had just risen substantially. There was no way she was going to trust the detective's investigative skills, and someone had to save her son's reputation. People were already canceling their reservations after learning about the demise of one of the guests. And an arrest, even if it were false, could ruin Nathan's business.

She started cutting the carrots again. Her mother's dining philosophy had given her an idea. For centuries, good food had been a key ingredient for breaking down barriers and getting people to talk—something she was determined to do with the guests and employees of the lodge. For her plan to work, sandwiches would never suffice. If she hurried, she just might be able to pull it off.

For the first time all morning Pricilla smiled,

because while cold cuts and cheese slices wouldn't hit the mark, she knew exactly what would.

———

Max jerked up in his chair then winced as a blast of pain shot through his ankle. "Pricilla?"

"Sorry. I didn't mean to disturb you." She set a small tray of snacks and sodas at the edge of a puzzle table Nathan had set up beside Max's chair on the front porch of the lodge. "Go back to sleep."

Max closed his eyes, but even with them shut, he could feel Pricilla's penetrating gaze on him.

He opened them again. "Where is everyone?"

"After a bit of persuading by Nathan, Detective Carter allowed Oscar to take the men fishing this morning. They should be back soon for lunch. Claire's sleeping, and Trisha's in her room reading. Nathan's still at the police station."

"I thought it seemed awfully quiet." He held up his hand to block the sun as she stood in front of him with her hands behind her back. "What's wrong?"

"Nothing that can't wait." She sat down and gripped the edges of the padded chair until her knuckles turned white. "It's really not that important."

While he'd never understand why Pricilla couldn't just get to the point, he doubted her blasé response came close to what she actually felt. He also knew her well enough to know that he'd never be able to sleep now. She'd stare at him until he gave her his full attention.

"Of course, it's important." He sat up and helped himself to a cracker and dip. "This is delicious. What is it?"

She loosened her grip on the armrest. "It's homemade liver pâté. I forgot about it with all that's happened. Thought you might be hungry."

Pâté? He frowned. He'd made it a rule to avoid anything that an animal had thought with, tasted with or. . .well, any other number of other unmentionable things. Still, he wasn't surprised at all that Pricilla could make even liver taste as good as filet mignon.

"I never thought I liked pâté, but this is wonderful." He took another scoop of the dip with his cracker and chuckled. "You know, I'd forgotten, but every year Violet used to bring homemade pâté to the church's Christmas party. She told me it was the one sophisticated recipe in her repertoire, which if you remember, was very limited."

"Was it good?"

He laughed at the memory. "I tried it one time and one time only. Violet had dozens of wonderful qualities, but cooking wasn't one of them. The year before she died, I found her uneaten pâté in the church trashcan. Saundra Huff caught me and made me promise to never tell Violet what she'd done, horrified she might hurt Violet's feelings. Saundra couldn't stand the idea of Violet taking her pâté home when no one had touched it. I never had the heart to tell her."

Pricilla's expression softened. "I'm glad you didn't."

"Me, too, but there's no telling how many years Saundra and the other women had been trying to save Violet's feelings."

"Everyone always loved Violet." She stared at the puzzle he'd started before deciding to take a nap and picked up one of the edges of the Thomas Kinkade picture. "Do you still miss her?"

He popped open the tab of his drink. "I'll always miss her, but I also know that it's time to move on."

He studied Pricilla's profile and caught the serious-ness in her expression. He couldn't stand the fact that she was unhappy, and he wanted to be the one to bring a smile to her face. Maybe it was time to tell her how he felt.

"You know, Pricilla, sometimes I think—"

He stopped.

With her focus on the puzzle, it was obvious that her mind was miles away, and besides, this wasn't the time to state his intentions. He couldn't really blame her. Obviously she was quite upset by the fact that Nathan was at this moment being questioned by Detective Carter. If the detective's interest had been in Trisha, or Pricilla for that matter, Max would be ready to engage the man in a duel.

A slight breeze tugged at the collar of his light jacket. He gazed out across the rugged terrain where the aspen trees had already begun to fade and would be bare by the end of the month. The ski resorts were still waiting for powder as the snowfall only reached the highest peaks of the mountains at this point. More than likely the coming snowstorms would more than make up for what was lacking right now. He never failed to be amazed at the wonder of God's beauty. And the stark contrast of man's behavior.

"Pricilla?"

She turned to him, brushing a silver curl away from her face. "I'm sorry. I must have missed the last thing you said."

"Never mind." He smiled. "I thought you hated puzzles."

"Normally I do." She picked up an edge piece and snapped it into place along the outer rim.

"It's Nathan, isn't it?"

She picked up another piece. "I'm worried."

"Me, too, but God convicted me of something this morning."

"What's that?" Looking up at him, she caught his gaze.

"No matter what is going on around us, He's our only true place of refuge. Admittedly, I've tried to rely on my own efforts for most of my life, but the older I get, the more I realize that it doesn't work that way."

Pricilla nodded and leaned back in her chair. "I always loved the verse that says, 'I will take refuge in the shadow of your wings until the disaster has passed.' But what if this disaster doesn't pass?"

"What do you mean?"

"What if they arrest Nathan and—"

"They're not going to arrest him."

"You don't know that." She picked up a cracker and nibbled on it. "What you think about Detective Carter?"

"What about him?" he asked.

"Do you think he knows what he's doing?"

"Of course he knows what he's doing. Otherwise, he wouldn't have been hired for the job."

"Don't you remember that his uncle's the sheriff?"

"So?" He knew where she was going with her line of questioning, but they couldn't just assume that Detective Carter had been hired simply as a favor to the family. This wasn't the Mafia, whose members stayed in the family business simply because of their last name.

Pricilla shook her head. "Carter could have got the position without being qualified. Max, this is serious. They've just taken Nathan down to the station for questioning. He could be arrested."

"They're not going to arrest him."

She let out a sigh. "Misty told me someone overheard him and Charles having an argument. Someone must have told the detective."

"Just because he argued with the man doesn't mean he killed him."

There was nothing like small towns when it came to letting rumors run loose. And Max knew that rumors could do as much, if not more, damage than the truth. But that didn't mean that questioning Nathan wasn't purely routine.

She leaned forward and caught his gaze. "Of course Nathan didn't kill him. You and I know that, but what about the detective?"

"I'm sure that the man is simply doing his job and looking into every angle—"

"My son's not an angle, and I don't intend for his reputation to be shredded to bits."

He took another sip of his drink. "You really don't like the detective, do you?"

"I've always had this second sense about people."

"Does this include your matchmaking skills?"

Pricilla frowned. "Detective Carter has more conceit than experience. A lethal combination if you ask me."

"Then what do you intend to do?"

"I intend to find out who murdered Charles Woodruff."

Max dropped his drink against the armrest, barely stopping it from tipping over. "You can't be serious." Except he knew she was.

"I'm very serious." Pricilla pulled a small notepad out of her apron pocket and flipped it open. "We need a list of suspects."

"Suspects? You know, you're starting to sound like the detective." She shot him a glaring look. "Sorry, go ahead."

"I've already made out a list of possible suspects that includes both lodge guests and workers. There's a total of ten. To save time, though, I've eliminated the two of us, as well as Nathan and Trisha. In each suspect, we're looking for secrets, a possible link to the crime, and, most importantly, a motive."

"What about opportunity?" He tried not to laugh. He couldn't believe he was going along with her scheme. But on the other hand, what other choice did he really have? "I like that one, because I have an alibi."

"I've already taken you off my list of suspects, but that's not necessarily true."

He frowned. "That I don't have an alibi?"

"If Charles was poisoned, say in his tea, we all had ample time to slip something into his mug."

Max considered her argument. "I suppose that's true—"

"But since I'm certain you for one did not murder Charles Woodruff, I'm not including you in my suspect list."

"Are you sure about that?"

"Max."

"Sorry." No matter how much he enjoyed teasing her, he supposed that now wasn't the time.

Pricilla skirted around the puzzle table and walked to the porch rail. "Suspect one, and the most obvious, of course, is Claire Woodruff, the victim's wife. She has an obvious link to the victim."

"As well as motive. Several heard them fighting."

Pricilla nodded and wrote something in her notebook. "We need to find out, then, what she's hiding. Next suspects. Simon Wheeler, Michael Smythe, and Anthony Mills."

"Three business men who had met Charles on a previous hunting trip."

"Great." Pricilla continued scribbling. "We've got our connection."

"Motive?"

"That's what we need to find out. Maybe they interact with Charles somehow in the business world. I'll make a note to follow up on that issue." She scribbled some notes and then tapped the pencil against the pad. "Next on the list is Oscar Philips. For starters, I don't like the man."

Max shook his head. "That's not applicable. Miss Marple may have had a certain intuition to solve a crime, as you say you have, but in real life, whether or not you like someone really doesn't count."

Pricilla pressed the notebook against her waist. "I didn't know you read mystery novels."

"I've always loved characters like Hercule Poirot and Sherlock Homes, but, as I just said, in the real world, what one thinks about a suspect really doesn't apply. It's always about the evidence."

She shot him a smile. "I think I've found myself quite a partner."

Max smiled back despite himself. Partners in crime would be more like it. While part of him was trying to figure out how to get her to lose interest in this ridiculous pursuit of justice, Max couldn't help but admire her determination. Her hazel eyes sparkled in the mid-morning sun, and no matter what her schemes might be to serve up justice in this situation, he knew he was hooked.

"So," Pricilla continued, "back to Oscar. He definitely knew Charles from coming to the lodge the past few years."

"You've got your link to the crime."

"And I'm sure he has a secret. Have you ever tried to really talk to him?"

He took another sip of his drink. "Can't say that I have."

"That's because you can't. He's evasive, shifty, suspicious—"

"And you, as I've said more than once, I'm sure, have an overactive imagination."

She cleared her throat as if dismissing his last comment. "Last on the list is Misty Majors. She has the same connection as Oscar, but that's all I have on her so far." Pricilla dropped the notebook and pen onto her chair and folded her arms across her chest. "What do you think?"

"Not bad." Max shifted in the chair and tried to find a more comfortable position for his foot. "You've got your list. Now what? It seems pretty full of holes to me."

"I'm afraid you're right. We're left with more questions than answers." She picked up the notebook and pen, tapped the pen against the pad, and cocked her head. "But I've already got that part figured out. Take in a deep breath."

He filled his lungs with the savory sent of lunch. "I smell food? What is it?"

Pricilla sat back down beside him. "My trump card. Herbed beef stew and a slice of my lemon crumb cake."

"That's your trump card?"

Pricilla smiled and nodded her head. "Think about it. One bite of my stew and the guests will open up, allowing me to fill in the blanks."

He lowered his brow, not convinced in the validity of her experiment. "That's your plan?"

"Do you like my pâté?"

"Excuse me?"

"My pâté. Do you like it?"

"It's delicious." He took another bite for emphasis. "But I already told you that."

She pointed a finger at him. "And that's not all you told me. One bite and you were telling me all about Violet's pâté and the secret of how everyone hated it—"

"Now wait a minute. I don't see how you can compare Violet's pâté with finding out who murdered Charles Woodruff."

"Why not? I need you to help me, Max."

"I don't know." He shook his head. "I'm worried that you're overdoing it for one thing, trying to get involved in an official investigation—"

"I'm fine, I promise."

Despite his best effort to stop Pricilla's harebrained idea, he knew there was no way out of this one.

"Please."

"On two conditions," he said, shaking his finger

at her like a stern headmaster. "You run every scheme of yours by me first, and everything you find out, you pass on to the detective."

She frowned, but nodded her head in agreement. He'd keep his promise to help her, but only to try and keep her out of trouble. Something he wasn't sure he'd actually be able to do.

7

Pricilla breathed in the spicy scent of her stew and smiled. She knew Max thought her idea to interview the guests was ridiculous, but she was convinced her plan was going to work. Lunch would be informal today, served in the smaller dining room that looked out across the mountains. She'd even sent Misty on an errand so the woman wouldn't get in the way of her investigation. Of course, Misty would have to be interviewed at some point as well, but Pricilla had that planned for later. All she needed now for her idea to work was simmering bowls of stew, hot yeast rolls, a listening ear—-and her suspects.

Standing in the corner of the room, she took a quick inventory of the table settings to make sure she hadn't forgotten anything. She still needed to put out the glasses and debated between the thick moose mugs or one of Nathan's latest purchases, eight-ounce tumblers with a colored drawing of the same animal on one side. Like every room in the lodge, this one had its own unique décor. From the moose tableware and faux antler utensils, to the antler chandelier hanging above the rustic table and the carved moose on the back of each chair—it was the setting any hunter or fisherman would love. She was counting on the relaxed atmosphere of the room to help ease her guests into a worthwhile conversation that would give her the answers she was looking for.

She turned toward the door as Max hobbled into the room, the rubber tips of his crutches thumping against the wood floor. He tottered for a moment then plopped down on a cowhide chair beside the crackling fireplace.

"Are you all right?" Forgetting the glasses, Pricilla hurried past the edge of the sideboard warmer to where he sat.

"I'm fine."

"But should you be up and around?"

"It's lunchtime." He flashed her a grin. "You know I can't resist your cooking."

"But you're not supposed to be in here. . . ." Pricilla stopped. While she didn't want to appear impolite, she also couldn't have her carefully laid plans infringed upon. The more people in the room, the less of a chance the guests would open up.

She caught his perplexed expression and frowned. "I'm sorry. I didn't mean it like that. It's just that—"

"Don't worry." The corners of his lips curled into a smile. "I just needed to stretch and thought you might want to know that the men are back from their fishing trip. Judging from the strong odor that passed by me a few minutes ago, I'm assuming they'll take a while to clean up."

Glancing at her watch, she decided on the tumblers and moved to place one at each setting. "Did they have a big catch?"

He shrugged and settled back into the chair. "You'll

have to ask them, but I got the impression that none of them were very happy. Which means—"

"They'll be less likely to open up."

Frustrated, Pricilla finished putting out the glasses and lifted the lid off the stew to stir the savory mixture. She'd done all she could do. Now it was a matter of praying her plan would unfold to her advantage. She might not uncover any dark secrets in the course of the next couple hours, but any hint as to the motive behind Charles Woodruff's demise would place her one step ahead of the detective. And it was far more likely that the guests would leak information to her before ever coming forward with clues for the detective.

Max tapped one of his crutches against the floor. "You're taking this far too seriously, Pricilla."

She turned to face him. "A man's dead and my son's been taken to the sheriff's office for questioning. I don't think anything I do from this point on is taking it too seriously."

"Come sit down." Max patted the ottoman in front of him.

She hesitated for a moment then placed the lid back on the warmer before crossing the room.

"Can I give you a few tips?" he asked.

She sat down and reached into her pocket. After thirty-plus years in the air force, he must have learned a thing or two about extracting information from the enemy. "Should I get out my notebook?"

"Not now." He reached out and squeezed her

hands. "The first step in any investigation is to relax. I want you to take a deep breath then let it out slowly."

Pricilla smiled and nodded her head. She couldn't resist his dimpled grin. Her heart felt like a jackhammer at a Seattle construction site, but she forced herself to close her eyes and take a deep breath. Strange. Not only was her heart pounding, but even with her eyes shut she felt dizzy. She opened her eyes. It had to be nerves. Who wouldn't be upset? Her son was right now being interrogated by the detective?

She couldn't smell the stew anymore. Instead, the scent of Max's cologne filled her senses. She'd never stopped to notice just how blue his eyes were. Blue like the color of the Colorado columbine. His hair had grayed but was still thick with a bit of curl around the ends. The saying that men aged gracefully was certainly correct in Max's case. Now that she thought about it, he'd only grown more handsome in the past few years.

She shook her head. How in the world had her thoughts shifted from her son's dilemma to the color of Max's eyes? Undoubtedly, she was feeling overly emotional today. After finding one dead body, making a false confession to murder, fearing for Max's life— and now her son's future—no wonder she felt as if she'd gone over the edge. Still, if she didn't know better, it would seem that her unbidden thoughts were leaning toward something romantic. But that was absurd. Max had always been. . .well. . .Max. Longtime friend, emotional support, and the one person who could always make Marty and her laugh. It had never mattered that his eyes reminded her of Paul Newman, or that his cologne left her head reeling.

She cleared her throat, and forced herself to refocus on the issue at hand. "What's step two?"

He shifted in the chair and readjusted his foot. "You've already completed step number two."

"I have?" Considering all her sleuthing knowledge came from books and TV shows, his statement pleased her. "And what would step two be?" she asked.

"Completing a factual analysis of the information surrounding the crime. In other words, what you have in your notebook for a start. A suspect list."

"And the next step?"

"Using your suspect list, find a viable motive behind Charles's murder."

Pricilla clenched her jaw. He was right. So she had a list of suspects and their connection to the crime. Unless she could gather more pertinent information from the guests, she'd be no help in ensuring her son didn't take the rap for the murder.

Ten minutes later, Max had left and Simon and Anthony were arriving, freshly showered from their morning fishing trip on Lake Paytah. With a brief explanation that Michael was not feeling well and wanted to skip lunch, they sat down at the end of the round table, and nodded when she set the bowls in front of them. Apparently they were hungry, because neither of them spoke as they dug into the thick stew.

She filled a plate with the hot rolls and set it before them. "How was the lake this morning, gentlemen?"

Simon grunted and took another bite of his stew.

She bustled around the table and handed them each an extra napkin. Apparently Max had been right that they weren't happy over the morning's trip. "Was it that bad?"

"Yep." Anthony's response was just as ambiguous.

Pricilla frowned. "Didn't you catch anything?"

"Nope."

Her eyes narrowed at Simon's curt response. She didn't want to hover over them like some bumbling private investigator, but in order to gather the information she needed, she was going to have to find a way to engage them in a discussion. This couldn't be a one-sided conversation, though at the moment she wondered if these men were capable of much more. Still, she had no intentions of giving up just because up to this point they'd only grunted or spoken in monosyllables.

She grabbed the water pitcher off the sideboard and topped off their already full glasses. Whether it was needed or not, she needed an excuse to stay in the room.

"Last time I went fishing with Nathan, we caught our limit of rainbow trout." She began serving another loaf of fresh bread. "Let me tell you, it was one of the tastiest meals I've ever had. Several of those trout were over twelve inches long. We fried them up and ate them with coleslaw and hushpuppies on the side. . . ."

Pricilla stopped talking.

Both men had dropped their spoons into their bowls and were staring at her as if she'd grown horns.

"Not *real* puppies, of course," she hurried on to explain. "My mother was from the South, and she always served those little fried dumplings of cornmeal. Normally you eat them with catfish, but. . ." Biting her lip, she stopped. She'd obviously wandered onto the wrong topic. "Anyway, I hope you like today's menu."

She dusted off her hands on her apron. This was getting absurd. They were going to be finished with their meal before she was able to add even a trace of evidence into her notebook. Trying to look busy, she wondered what she could say to get them to talk. Frankly, if she could do things her way, she'd opt to find a small room with a bald light and use more forceful tactics. Just because such methods were considered extreme, why beat around the bush when the truth might be easily discovered with a bit of creativity?

She piled a second plate with hot bread then placed it on the table in front of the men, contemplating what to say next. While it was true that subtlety had never been her strongest point, she was certain that her cooking would eventually make up for any problems she might encounter in getting the men to talk. Even if she hadn't served fresh fish.

"Sad thing about Mr. Woodruff, isn't it?" she began, trying once again to fuel the dying conversation.

"Yep" was the only response she got. She needed a question that couldn't be answered with a simple yes or no. Or, in their case, no yeps and grunts.

Pretending to brush crumbs off the tablecloth, Pricilla reached out to straighten one of the silverware settings. "Did either of you know him well?"

Anthony wiped his mouth with a napkin. "The three of us went hunting with him once."

At last a complete sentence. She decided to push for more. "What was he like? I didn't really know the man at all except for a brief exchange before his untimely passing."

Simon looked to his friend. "Pretty quiet, wouldn't you say?"

"Yep. He was pretty quiet. Kept to himself."

While she couldn't really call it progress, at least she had them talking. "I understand you both are businessmen. Did you ever meet him in a professional capacity?"

She didn't miss the look that passed between the two men, nor the silent pause that followed her question.

Anthony reached for another piece of bread, his face void of expression. "You obviously haven't heard about the man's reputation. He wasn't exactly the kind of person one chooses to do business with. Always cutthroat and out to win, no matter what."

Unable to take notes, Pricilla told herself to find out more about this hunting trip of theirs. For whatever reason, the men obviously harbored bad feelings toward Mr. Woodruff. Whether or not they'd go into greater detail was another question.

"I understand you own a. . .dot-com company," she continued, hoping she'd phrased it correctly. With technology advancing as rapidly as it did, she found it amazing how anyone could keep up with what was going on. She was probably one of the few remaining holdouts of the modern world who still didn't have her own computer or e-mail account.

"We did," Simon quipped. "Sold it a few years back for a nice profit."

"We're preparing to launch a new online consulting business in the next few months."

Anthony's addition gave her little to go on. "Is that how you first met up with Mr. Woodruff? In business circles, I mean."

The two men didn't have to say anything for Pricilla to realize that she'd pushed them too far.

"Now listen here." Simon shoved his bowl away from the edge of the table then scooted back his chair. "I'll be the first to admit that I didn't like the man, but that doesn't mean that I killed him."

"Same here." Anthony folded his arms across his chest and eyed her warily. "Did the detective set you up to ask us about our relationship with Charles?"

Pricilla wanted to laugh at the question. If only they knew the real motivation behind her line of questioning, they'd more than likely turn her over to the detective.

She waved her hand into the air and tried to shrug aside the comment. "Just curious is all."

The men rose from the table and mumbled their thanks for the lunch as they left the room. The interview was over. Clearing their dirty dishes from the table, Pricilla prepared the table for the next guests, hoping that whoever once said that curiosity killed the cat had been mistaken.

Max slipped into the dining room, amused at the interchange he'd overheard between Pricilla and the men. While he had to admit her plan did have merit, she obviously picked the wrong two men to start off with. He chuckled to himself. One had to give her credit. He'd been involved in literally hundreds of official interviews throughout his career as an officer and not once had anyone had the idea to offer a homemade meal in order to get the conversation to flow. Obviously, the problem had been Pricilla's rusty interviewing tactics and not the food.

Pricilla placed her hand against her chest when she saw him. "How long have you been standing there?"

"Long enough to hear the end of your conversation with the men."

"They didn't even try the cake." Pricilla's expression fell. "It didn't exactly go as smoothly as I'd intended."

Max leaned against the end of the table. "What if I interrogate the next suspect?"

"I thought you were against all of this."

He hobbled his way around the table to one of the chairs and sat down. "I am, but it's starting to rain, and I've worked on the puzzle until I can't see straight with my bifocals anymore. And besides all that, I'm hungry. Who's left on your list?"

"Michael, Claire—"

"Misty." Max smiled as the young woman entered the room. No time like the present to show Pricilla firsthand a thing or two about how to handle a proper interview. "I was just sitting down to eat. Would you care to join me?"

He ignored Pricilla's glare as the young woman set a package down at the end of the table. "I'm flattered for the offer, Mr. Summers, but I'm just here to give Mrs. Crumb the package I picked up in town for her. Besides, it's probably not appropriate for me to be eating with one of the guests."

"She's quite right, Max." Pricilla nodded her head. "And I hadn't really planned—"

"It's not a problem at all." He reached for a piece of bread and spread on some butter. "Who wants to bother with formalities? I hate to eat alone."

With hunting now out of the picture and the detective's directive that they all stay near the lodge, it didn't hurt to have something to occupy his time. Eating at the table with Misty, and whoever else showed up, was bound to break down barriers. Besides, how difficult could an undercover interview with an attractive young woman be?

8

Pricilla frowned as Misty took a seat across the table from Max. While she couldn't complain about the housekeeper's efficiency, allowing the staff to eat with the guests was not acceptable. What if someone joined them while Misty, their housekeeper, was sitting at the table, eating and laughing like one of the paying guests? Certainly Nathan would hold to the same standards, believing it wasn't the impression a top-rated lodge should ever leave.

She placed two bowls of steaming stew in front of Max and Misty but this time didn't smile at the savory scent wafting through the room.

Max smiled up at her. "This looks delicious, Pricilla. Thank you."

"And thank you, Mr. Summers, for inviting me to join you." Misty put her napkin in her lap, clearly thrilled to have been asked to stay for lunch. "While the food is always wonderful, today's company simply can't be beat."

"Please, why don't you call me Max?"

"And you can call me Misty."

The housekeeper laughed, or rather, she giggled like a schoolgirl on a date. Pricilla's brow puckered. Certainly the young woman wasn't flirting with Max? He was over twice her age.

"I'd hoped for the chance to chat with you at some point during the week," Misty said between spoonfuls.

"Really?" Max sat back in his chair.

"I always find older men so much more interesting than those my own age."

Max winked at Pricilla as she set a plate of hot bread on the table, but the gesture did little to erase her growing irritation.

So this was how he ran his investigations with attractive younger women? Put on the charm like Cary Grant and then sit back and watch it all unfold? The way Misty was opening up under his well-seasoned plan, he would have the case solved by the end of the meal. Clearly she didn't need to be a part of this.

Pricilla cleared her throat. "I need to check on some things in the kitchen. If you need seconds, there is plenty of food on the sideboard."

"Why don't you join us, Mrs. Crumb?" Misty asked.

Why did *Mrs. Crumb* sound so old-fashioned and downright ancient coming from Misty—whose pert smile and bright blue eyes lit up her wrinkle-free face like a ripe peach?

Pricilla forced a smile across her lips. "Thank you, but I want to make sure that things are ready for tonight's meal."

Max waved his hand in the air without looking up. "Then don't worry about us. We'll be fine."

"I'll be in to help you shortly." Misty patted Max's hand, a gesture Pricilla didn't miss. "And I'll be sure and take good care of Max in the meantime."

Pricilla picked up the package and hurried toward the kitchen, wondering why, all of a sudden, there was a lump the size of the Rocky Mountains in her throat. Maybe she would have done better with her own investigation if she'd tried buttering up the men before launching her questions, but one didn't have to be so obvious.

Pricilla pulled a stack of cloth napkins out of the bottom kitchen drawer and began running the taupe material through iron napkin rings she'd found at one of the local shops. Surely she wasn't feeling jealous. She and Max had known each other for years, and she'd never looked at him as anything more than a close friend. Just because Misty was pretty, jovial, and less than half her age—okay, far less than half her age—didn't mean that the girl was interested in Max. She was simply being friendly.

Once again, it had to be the stress. It was true that Max had always been there for her, flying in when her husband died and sending frequent letters as he could truly sympathize with her after losing his own wife. He'd been there to give her spiritual advice when she needed it and sent her small gifts on her birthday and for Christmas. But if it was nothing more than friendship she felt toward him, then why did her heart pound when she pictured Max's dimpled smile? And why did her heart sink when the housekeeper had his full attention?

"Mrs. Crumb?"

Pricilla set down the last napkin and turned around as Trisha walked into the room. "Did you get some rest?"

"Sort of." The young woman plopped down on a bar stool before resting her chin in her hands. "I thought reading would distract me, but I've read the same page at least a dozen times, and I couldn't tell you a thing of what I read. So much for the back cover's claims to grab my attention from page one and not let go until the last sentence."

"I'm sure it's not the book." Pricilla joined her at the counter, mirroring Trisha's glum expression. "I understand completely. This whole situation has left me on edge, and now with Nathan down at the sheriff's office. . ."

Trisha slid off her chunky bracelet and rolled it between her fingers. "I know you're worried about him. It's strange. I've known Nathan for just a matter of days but there's this connection between us. Maybe it's just because you and Dad have always been close."

Or maybe it was something much deeper. Pricilla smiled despite the somber mood of the day. No matter what was going on around them, she still believed firmly that Nathan and Trisha were right for each other. All they needed were a few more nudges in the right direction and human nature would take care of the rest.

"I checked on Claire before coming down," Trisha said.

"How is she?" Pricilla pulled a bag of red and green peppers from the fridge and laid them beside the cutting board, mentally calculating how much she should chop for tonight's antipasto pasta salad.

"I tried to convince her to let me bring her some lunch, but she wasn't interested."

Pricilla frowned. "Surely I can come up with something tempting to whet her appetite. I know it's difficult, but she has to eat. I'll take something up to her in a little bit."

Trisha took a piece of red pepper and popped it into her mouth. "I'm afraid she thinks the detective suspects her."

Pricilla rested her knife against the board. "What do you think?"

"I don't know." Trisha scrunched her lips together. "I suppose being the spouse of a murdered man makes one an automatic suspect. She did tell me she was Charles's beneficiary, and, from what I gathered, has a lot to gain financially from his death."

"And from the way everyone seems to have disliked him, perhaps she didn't have much to lose." Pricilla closed her mouth, wanting to bite back her words. "I'm sorry. I shouldn't have said that."

"Don't worry. I'm sure we've all thought that a time or two. If he was murdered, as the authorities believe, someone obviously didn't like him."

"I suppose you're right."

Pricilla went back to chopping the peppers. She knew little about Charles Woodruff, and speaking ill of the man would gain nothing. Money was always a possible motive, and she needed to add it to her notebook once she was done making her salad.

Trisha leaned back, stretching the muscles in her shoulders. "Do you know where my dad is?"

Pricilla scowled. Here was a subject she'd like to avoid. "He's in the dining room, eating lunch with Misty."

"With Misty?"

"I had the brilliant idea to see if we could find out more about Charles and his relationship with the guests. He chose Misty."

Trisha cocked her head. "If I didn't know better, I'd say you almost sound a bit. . .jealous?"

"Of course not." Pricilla dismissed the idea. "It's just the stress of this whole ordeal has me feeling a bit off. Aren't you planning to eat something?"

"I'm not really hungry. What's for lunch?"

"Stew, hot yeast rolls, and lemon crumb cake."

Trisha mulled over her choices. "Is there any cereal and milk? On any other day, I'd go nuts for a bowl of homemade stew, especially with the takeout I eat everyday, but—"

"Don't worry. I understand." Pricilla waved her hand in front of her. "If you look in the pantry, I'm sure you'll find something you like."

"Thanks." Trisha snatched a spoon from the silverware drawer then headed for the pantry. "I'll grab myself a bowl of cereal then give my book another try."

Pricilla dumped the peppers into the large fluted bowl she'd already filled with pasta, sausage, tomatoes, and cheeses. All she needed to make now was the dressing. Standing in front of the cupboard, she pulled out the balsamic vinegar then rested her hands against the smooth counter as Trisha left the room.

She couldn't stand it any longer. What was Misty telling Max? Despite the ridiculous pangs of jealousy she may or may not be experiencing, the truth was, Misty might hold information that might be valuable in solving the crime—and possibly saving her son. Slamming the cupboard door shut, she hurried back down the hall and planted herself outside the doorway of the dining room. Eavesdropping might not be the most ethical behavior, but as someone somewhere once said, desperate times call for desperate measures.

—

Max knew he was making progress. He took another bite of the stew and listened to Misty who was obviously familiar with the guests, knew things the rest of them might never find out. While he was never one to sit around and gossip, today his purpose was to extract as much information as he could regarding Charles Woodruff's relationship to the other guests— as resourcefully as possible.

He wiped his chin with his napkin and leaned back in his chair. "You must know a lot about the ins and outs of the lodge as well as the guests, Misty. You've been working here for. . .how many years?"

"I started working here eight years ago last July. It's hard to believe that much time has passed." Misty sighed, fiddling with her spoon. "My husband left me when my girls were still in diapers. They're nine and ten now. Don't know what I would have done if Nathan hadn't hired me. Out of work with only a high school education. Makes life difficult."

He helped himself to another roll then reached for the butter dish. "Seems like you've done well for yourself."

She nodded. "The job came with a cabin that's become home, and who can complain about waking up to a view of the Rocky Mountains every morning?"

Max took a sip of his drink, ready to push the conversation a step further. "You knew Charles Woodruff from years past. What's your take on all of this? Do you really think that one of us could have bumped him off?"

"It is hard to imagine, isn't it?" Misty giggled again. "Did you know the man had false teeth?"

"Really?" His eyes widened, but he mirrored her grin. "Not a motive for murder, I don't suppose."

"Of course not, but I could tell you things—"

"Let's stick to things regarding the case for now." On the surface, Misty didn't seem to be hiding anything.

In the long run, he calculated, direct questions would get the most information out of her.

"Okay." Misty leaned forward in her seat as if she were afraid someone else might be listening. "Here's an interesting fact, then. Charles bought out Simon Wheeler and Anthony Mill's failing business a few months ago. Makes you wonder what kind of hard feelings there might have been between them."

Bingo.

Max knew he was onto something, but he kept his expression neutral. "That is interesting. I wonder what circumstances surrounded the buyout?"

"From what I heard, it wasn't a pleasant takeover." Misty fiddled with the edge of her napkin. "Just my opinion, of course, but I could definitely sense animosity between Charles and those men. And I certainly don't think they intended to come here at the same time either. I overheard there was a conflict with the Woodruffs' original reservation and they had to change it at the last minute."

Max rubbed his chin with the tips of his fingers. Pricilla was going to be pleased with what he was coming up with. It might not be anything, but he'd learned from experience never to ignore information, no matter how minute. Had one of them been planning to knock off Charles, or had it been a spur of the moment decision when they found out he was staying at the lodge? Either way, the men already had a connection to the victim, and now they had a motive.

"Enough about Charles and the other men." Misty swung her long hair behind her shoulder. "If you ask me, they're all nothing more than stuffy businessmen who care more about making money than who they step on. As for me—"

Max tried to interpret the gleam in her eye. "What about you?"

"I'm looking for someone much more stable. Someone older who realizes that there's much more to life than earning a fortune or stomping on other people to get ahead. . . Someone like you."

Max swallowed hard. Surely she wasn't implying that she was interested in him? He was imagining things. Of course he was. He felt something pat his foot, and he froze. Had he just bumped the edge of the table leg, or was it Misty?

"I, um. . ." What could he say? "Can I get you a piece of Pricilla's lemon crumb cake?" He scooted back from the table and then winced, remembering his sprained foot.

Misty laughed as she moved around the table. "I think you'd better let me get it."

He watched out of the corner of his eye while she served up two thick slices of the cake, with its rich, lemony frosting. At least Pricilla was nowhere near. He'd sensed before she left the room that she hadn't been happy with him eating lunch with Misty, though he wasn't sure why. Unless she could be. . .jealous.

The thought was highly unlikely, but he smiled

anyway, liking the idea that Pricilla might actually have feelings for him. Misty set a piece of cake in front of him, and he took a big bite of the moist treat. Maybe there was hope for him and Pricilla after all. But he still had to deal with Misty.

He ate his cake in silence, trying to avoid Misty's steady gaze.

"How long do you plan on staying at the lodge?" she asked after a minute had passed. "I understand you've recently retired."

Max coughed, wondering what her questions were leading to. "Yes, I was in the air force."

"Wow." He might as well have told her he was an astronaut or the president of the United States. She looked just as impressed. "I've never been able to resist a man in uniform. There's just something about those starched collars and shiny buttons that leave me completely breathless. Crazy, isn't it? I'd love to see you in your uniform—"

"You know, Misty, it's been wonderful eating lunch with you, but I—" He shoved his plate away from the edge of the table, avoiding her fervent gaze. "Time for my afternoon nap, you know."

He groaned as he rose from the table. Not so much from his throbbing foot, but more in an attempt to emphasis the age difference between them. Surely Misty saw him as practically ancient.

"Let's do it again then, soon." Misty's eyes hadn't lost their gleam. "I'd love to hear all about your military experiences. It sounds so. . .so manly."

Max tried not to choke. Misty's interest had nothing to do with the suspects or the recent murder and everything to do with him. Throwing his napkin on the table, he hobbled out of the room like a coon with his tail on fire.

9

By the time Pricilla saw Max round the corner, it was too late. He slammed into her, the rubber knob on the bottom of his crutch jamming against the end of her shoe and barely missing her toes.

"Max!" Pricilla pressed her back against the wall, thankful neither of them had fallen. Feeling young at heart would do little to curb the probable injuries of such an accident. Max's fall this morning was proof of that. "What in the world are you doing?"

"I could ask you the same thing." A streak of pain reflected in the corner of his eyes, as he must have bumped his sore ankle, but she also didn't miss the hint of amusement they held. He knew exactly what she had been doing.

"Eavesdropping?" His grin spoke volumes.

"What happened?" Misty bustled around the corner, saving Pricilla from answering his question. "Are you both all right?"

Misty looked straight at her.

"Yes. I was just. . ." Pricilla tugged at the bottom of her red tunic in an attempt to get her composure back. She certainly couldn't confess she'd been eavesdropping on their conversation. At least not to Misty.

"Just a bit of a collision," Max said, coming to her rescue. "Why don't we go sit on the porch for a while, Pricilla? This old man's tired."

Pricilla stifled a laugh. While eavesdropping, she hadn't missed Misty's clear advances or Max's attempts to thwart them. Having to take a nap was a ready excuse she found extremely amusing.

"Are you sure you're all right?" Misty still looked worried.

"We're fine. Really." Pricilla blew out a short breath. If Misty had been the one to discover her spying, she'd never have lived it down. Thankfully, she only had to deal with Max.

Misty shrugged. "If you're sure, I guess I'll head for the kitchen and make sure everything is cleaned up for this evening."

"Good idea, Misty." Even Max appeared relieved that she was leaving.

Any feelings of jealousy Pricilla had once entertained had dissipated and were replaced with amusement. While the idea of Misty coming on to Max seemed ridiculous, it was even more ridiculous to think that Max might go along with it. Hadn't Pricilla known him long enough to know that his integrity was far too great for him to falsely encourage someone—even during an "investigation"?

Pricilla followed Max outside into the afternoon sunlight and breathed in the sharp scent of the surrounding pine trees. How she could have ever managed to be jealous of Misty, she couldn't imagine.

Max laid his crutches against the wall and slid awkwardly into his favorite chair. "How much of our conversation did you overhear?"

Pricilla raised her voice a notch in an attempt to imitate Misty's higher pitched tone. "I've never been able to resist a man in uniform. I'd love to see yours—"

"Please." He rubbed his temples with his fingers and shook his head. "I don't remember the last time I've felt so embarrassed."

"Why? You should feel honored. She's young and beautiful, and in reality a very sweet girl."

He held up his hand in defense. "A sweet girl who needs to find someone her own age."

Pricilla felt the wheels in her mind begin to spin at the comment. Things were turning out well between Trisha and Nathan so far; what if—

"Don't even go there, Pricilla."

"Go where?" She tried to shoot him an innocent look, but he obviously didn't buy it.

"A love match for Misty." He pointed his finger at her and shook his head. "You've forgotten how well I know you. You see a damsel in distress and immediately send out the call for Prince Charming."

"That's not true—"

"Isn't it?"

She avoided his gaze this time. He did know her far too well. Penelope jumped up into her lap and began purring, giving Pricilla something to focus on other than Max's intense gaze.

Max cleared his throat. "I came up with a motive for you."

Pricilla couldn't help but grin. He obviously didn't want to discuss Misty anymore, and she was glad. Neither did she. Still, she couldn't help but be relieved that Max cared less about Misty's advances, though why it even mattered to her in the first place she wasn't quite sure. There was nothing wrong with Max finding love again. Quite the contrary. Wasn't it true that most couples who had satisfying marriages more often than not went on to marry again after one of them died? On the other hand, marriage at her age seemed far too complicated for some reason. She shook her head. Max was right. It was time to change the subject.

"I overheard something about Simon and Anthony's business?"

He let out a low chuckle at her confession. "Interesting, isn't it? I'm still trying to connect the dots. The three of them sold their online business for a huge profit, and then Simon and Anthony turned around and lost everything to Charles. But how?"

"There are never any guarantees in the business world. One day a millionaire, the next day bankrupt." Pricilla leaned against the thick cushions of the chair and stared down the empty road that lead to the lodge. She glanced at her watch. It was almost two o'clock and Nathan still wasn't home. Her worry was escalating into full-fledged anxiety.

Max tapped his fingers against the arm of the chair. "I thought I'd do a bit of research online from Nathan's computer once he returns. Maybe I'll find out something."

Trying to push aside her worry for her son, she pulled out her notebook, wondering now if she should have signed up for the computer class that had been offered to their Golden Oldies group at church last spring. Up to this point, she'd never thought that a machine could actually be an ally. In her opinion, computers ended up making people work harder rather than ease the burden of labor. She'd always seen the contraption as one of man's unidentifiable enemies—too complicated, too time consuming, and too antisocial.

She flipped the notebook open and jotted down a reminder to talk to Claire about the takeover. Computers might be out of her league, but she could deal with pen and paper. "I can't help you with any online research, but I will speak to Claire about her husband's business. She should know something."

Whether or not Claire would tell her was another issue.

"I have to be honest, Pricilla. After today's experience, I'm even more convinced that we really should leave this to Detective Carter." Max fiddled with the zipper on his jacket. "No matter how valid your motivation to get involved, this isn't our business. It's simply too dangerous. It's not a military investigation or even a civilian issue. This is a murder investigation that needs to be handled correctly by the authorities."

Pricilla frowned, disagreeing with his assessment. It *was* their business. Or at least hers. She'd never been one to let an injustice go, and she wouldn't start now. True, murder was out of her league, but with a little creativity. . .

"Maybe we need to try a different approach," she offered.

"Like what? You were subtle, I was blunt, and neither approach got us very far."

She didn't like the way the conversation was headed. She knew Max had never been of the opinion that what she was doing was appropriate, but up until now he'd at least gone along with her ideas—harebrained as they might be at times.

"I don't know." She felt uneasy under his intense gaze. "I'm not content to sit around and wait for the detective to arrest someone. Especially if that someone is innocent."

"You're worrying again. I still say we step back completely, and let the authorities handle things."

Pricilla frowned. He might be right, but that didn't lessen her resolve to do what she could to find out the truth. It wasn't as if she thought Nathan would actually be in trouble with the law. No one in his right mind would ever seriously entertain the thought that Nathan could have done such a vile act, and certainly not if they really knew him. Maybe that was part of her fear. The detective was new to the department and didn't know Nathan. The facts said someone overheard her son arguing with the victim shortly before the murder took place. That's what the detective would focus on.

Nathan's pickup truck spun into the circular drive. After parking the vehicle at an odd angle in front of the lodge, he slid out from the driver's side, worry lines clearly marking his forehead.

His boots clattered up the front steps. "I'll be in my office if anyone needs me."

Pricilla jumped as the screen door slammed shut behind him. "I take it things didn't go well."

Max squeezed her hand. "They didn't arrest him. He probably just needs to cool off."

"Slight comfort when you know that the detective could still show up any minute and arrest him."

"I've told you before, and I firmly believe it. They're not going to arrest your son."

Pricilla glanced at the house. "I'm going inside to talk to him."

"He looked like he wanted to be left alone."

She headed for the front door. "He's my son. I don't have to leave him alone."

Pricilla knocked on the doorframe of Nathan's office before entering. He sat in his chair with his eyes closed, as if he were trying to compose himself.

"Do you want me to come back later?" Despite her last words to Max, she did respect her son's privacy. But that didn't lessen her desire to fix everything for him.

He opened his eyes and rested his hands on the

desktop. "Come in and shut the door."

She closed the door behind her then sat across from him in a pine chair that matched the rest of the office's rustic decor. "What happened?"

Her son tapped his hands against the desk and breathed in deeply. "Before I get to our friend Detective Carter, I just got off the phone with a TV news producer from clear across the state. I told him the same thing I told our little newspaper and, luckily, no one knows yet that Charles was murdered. But it's only a matter of time."

"I'm sorry, Nathan. I'm sure it will all work out. God's in control, despite what it looks like to us," said Pricilla. "Now, what about your talk with Carter?"

"In his typically brusque manner, he asked an assortment of questions, like my relationship with Charles and the lodge's financial situation." He paused. "I'm trying to see things from the authorities' point of view, but it's hard."

"What do you mean?"

Nathan shook his head. "I see now why you don't like Detective Carter."

She cringed inside at the comment. While his statement was true, she really had tried to keep the opinion to herself. "Were my feelings that obvious?"

"Aren't they always?"

Pricilla had to laugh. She'd never been accused of being ambiguous. "Tell me about your argument with Charles."

His face hardened into a scowl. "I'll be the first to admit that it was a bit heated, but Charles was an arrogant man who never accepted anything less than what he wanted."

"And he didn't get it this time?"

"It was out of the question. He wanted a different guide. No explanations, just a different guide or this would be his last year supporting my lodge."

Pricilla mulled over the new information. "A strange request."

"Especially considering the fact that Oscar is my best guide and has gone with Charles in the past with no problems that I'm aware of. You'd have to know Charles, though, to fully understand."

"What do you mean?" Pricilla refrained from pulling out her notebook again. She didn't know how this latest tidbit of information fit into the larger scope of things, but she was determined to find out.

Nathan picked up a pen and tapped the end against a blank pad of paper. "To put it nicely, he was high maintenance. He's been coming for the past five or six years, and every year it's the same thing. He complained at the drop of a hat, always insisted on special meal requests, and frankly, never had anything nice to say to anyone."

"Why didn't you just refuse him a room, then? Say you were booked or make up some sort of excuse."

"Believe me, I considered that seriously, but normally the man brought several people with him, and I couldn't afford to turn down that kind of business. Often those he invited came back the next year on their own. So whatever I thought about the man personally, he was good for business."

Not anymore.

Pricilla let out a deep sigh and tried to make heads or tails out of the information. She might hate jigsaws, but this was a puzzle she was determined to solve. All she needed was a bit of patience and the pieces would eventually come together.

Nathan cleared his throat and flipped on his computer. "This year his wife booked, and I couldn't say no. Even though it was just the two of them. Some sort of marital retreat, she told me."

"Surely an argument with Charles couldn't be considered grounds as a motive for murder. I mean, you'd think they'd have to come up with something a bit more solid."

Nathan rubbed the back of his neck with his hand while the monitor warmed up. "While I think I convinced the detective that I had nothing to do with Charles's death, I can't be sure. The man seems to think he's an updated version of Columbo."

Pricilla chuckled at the image. "So he actually thinks you're capable of murder?"

He shrugged. "Who knows what the man is thinking, but to his credit, he's thorough. I have a feeling he's trying to please his uncle, or at least live up to the older man's solid reputation."

"And going about it all the wrong way." She pulled out her notebook, unable to stop herself anymore. She scribbled yet another question regarding the conflict between Oscar and Charles. Unfortunately, her questions were beginning to far outweigh any answers she might have come up with.

"What's that?"

"This?" She tapped the thin pad on her leg and smiled at him. "Just keeping my own notes of what's going on. I refuse to have your name marred because the detective was in too much of a hurry to solve the case. What about Claire, for instance? Surely she'd have a stronger motive than you and warrants a ride downtown. I've heard there was a life insurance policy involved—"

"Mom, please don't tell me you've become a Jessica Fletcher wannabe?"

She avoided his sharp gaze. "Okay, I won't."

"Have you?"

A knock on the door stopped her from answering his question.

"Come in."

Pricilla hated the fatigue in her son's voice, but didn't miss the way his eyes lit up when Trisha stepped into the room.

"Sorry to interrupt—"

"No, please come in, Trisha." Nathan stood and offered her a chair next to Pricilla.

Trisha tugged on the gauzy sleeve of her vintage-looking blouse and sat down. "I saw your truck parked outside and wanted to know how things went."

He took a seat and straightened out his arms in front of him. "No handcuffs yet."

Trisha smiled. "I guess that's a good sign."

Pricilla didn't miss the strong currents that had vibrated across the room at Trisha's entrance. They might not see it yet, but she was certain that it wasn't going to take much more pushing on her end for this relationship to blossom into something serious. "Nathan, I have an idea."

He raised his brows in a silent question.

"Take Trisha fishing for the rest of the afternoon." She shoved the notebook back into her pocket, her mind having shifted to a much more pleasant pursuit. "You might not catch anything, but at least you'll be away from the lodge for a while. You need a break and things are quiet here."

He rubbed his chin. "I don't know—"

Trisha sat forward, looking uncomfortable. "Please don't feel pressured on my account—"

"Trust me, the idea is appealing." Nathan's smile lit up his eyes. "And it's even more appealing if you'd agree to come with me. It's just that—"

"That what?" Pricilla felt determined not to let a murder investigation hinder any chances of the two of them getting together.

He stared at the computer screen. "Besides needing to catch up on this month's accounting, I guess I'm just worried about not being here if something else happens—"

"Nothing else will happen," Pricilla interrupted. "Max and I will be here with Misty. What could go wrong?"

"What could go wrong?" Nathan eyed her curiously. "What hasn't gone wrong?"

Pricilla pressed her lips together. Perhaps it wasn't the most logical question to ask, considering all that had happened in the past forty-eight hours, but still. . .

Nathan stood and leaned against the desk with his palms. "Are you up to it, Trisha? Despite the fact that everything seems to be falling down around us with no end in sight, my mom's right. I really could use a break."

"Do I dare admit I've never been fishing in my life?" She shot him a sheepish grin.

"You've never been fishing?"

"I thought I'd hinted earlier that I'm not exactly the outdoor type. I'm willing to attempt a go of it, though."

"A positive attitude and one of my fishing rods are all you'll need." Nathan walked around the desk toward Trisha. "And you're sure you don't mind, Mom?

"Not at all."

"You can call me on my cell phone if you need anything."

Pricilla smiled as the two stepped out of the office. Murder or not, there was no reason to put aside her matchmaking plans. And besides, she had plans herself.

With tonight's dinner ready for the grill, she had just enough time to go upstairs and have a heart-to-heart chat with Charles's widow.

10

Pricilla set the hot bowl of stew on the wicker tray then paused for a moment to make sure she hadn't forgotten anything. Despite her earlier failure in using comfort food to extract information during her interrogation, she still believed her idea had merit. And if nothing else, it was her Christian duty. Claire Woodruff had been through a horrifying ordeal. Bringing her a meal was the least Pricilla could do.

"Pricilla?"

She turned sharply, paying for it with a piercing pain that shot through her hip. "You scared me, Max."

He folded his arms across his chest and leaned against the counter. "Hmm. . .jumpy and a bit on edge. Seems suspicious to me."

She frowned at the comment. "I thought I'd been eliminated from the suspect list."

"Then let's look again at the facts." Max hobbled toward her, a wide grin across his face. "You now hold a tray filled with an assortment of mouthwatering treats. Because of the fancy tea cloth, we'll deduce that it is for a woman. Now, I just spoke to Trisha who was on her way to go fishing with Nathan, a fact that I plan to return to in just a minute, by the way. Misty's already eaten, as we both know. So. . .that leaves Claire, number one suspect on the detective's list—and most likely in your book as well."

Pricilla cleared her throat. "She's a woman who needs a friend. And a good home-cooked meal to keep up her strength won't hurt either."

She held up her head in mock challenge. It wasn't a lie. Not even a stretch of the truth if one thought about it. The woman had just lost her husband.

"All of that might be true, but"—he pointed to the pocket of her tunic, which held her notebook—"you can't tell me that you didn't plan to ask a few pointed questions while you're up there."

"Only if the opportunity arises. She might need someone to talk to." *Or someone to confess to,* though she wouldn't dare say that aloud.

Deciding to add a piece of her cake to the tray, she took down a saucer from the cupboard and cut a thick slice of the dessert. She did have a list of questions she wanted to ask the woman, and while she very well might not get the chance, she planned to at least try. She believed Claire held the key to much of the investigation, and unless she had been totally oblivious to her husband's work, she had to know something about Charles's relationship with Anthony and the other men.

Max picked up the knife she left on the platter and cut himself a thin piece of cake. "I'm not going to convince you to stop your investigation, am I?"

"Nope." She set the saucer on the tray. She didn't want to argue with him, but she couldn't deny her convictions either. It was time to change the subject. "I thought you were taking a nap."

"I'm still going to. There's one other thing I want to talk to you about first. Nathan and Trisha."

Pricilla frowned. Surely he hadn't changed his mind about their matchmaking scheme.

"I don't know if you had a hand in things," he began before she had a chance to defend herself, "but my daughter's going fishing."

She couldn't read his expression. "And that's a. . . good thing?" She might as well hope for the best in a situation like this.

"Yes, it is." Now, Max's smile reached his eyes. "You know Trisha. She loves the opera, museums, and designer clothes. To get a man to convince her to wear jeans and an old shirt and go fishing. . .well, the girl's smitten, if you ask me."

Pricilla laughed and picked up the tray. At least one of her plans was headed in the right direction. Maybe she could go into the matchmaking business if her stint as an amateur detective didn't pay off.

"So you're not opposed to my matchmaking attempts?"

"I definitely think you should stick with those skills rather than your detective work. In the long run, you're liable to get into a lot less trouble. Murder is permanent."

Pricilla shuddered. He was right. Murder was a serious offense, especially considering the likelihood that someone currently staying under this roof had executed the deadly plan.

Max said good luck as she left the kitchen, and five minutes later Pricilla knocked gently on the door of the Elk Room, where Nathan had moved Claire after her husband's passing. She entered when she heard a soft "come in."

Claire lay on top of the elk-print duvet, dressed in a plush terry-cloth robe and pink slippers.

"I thought you might be hungry." Pricilla set the tray on the pine nightstand beside the bed, careful not to knock over Claire's pill bottles, and sent up a short prayer for wisdom. She was definitely going to need it.

Claire rubbed her swollen eyes then closed the book on her lap and set it aside. "I don't know if I can eat—"

"You have to. I know it's difficult, but you won't be able to do anything if you don't keep up your strength." Pricilla folded her hands together, hoping she could find a way to convince the woman not only to eat something, but to open up to her as well. "Do you mind if I stay for a few minutes? It might help to have someone to talk to."

Claire shrugged. "Let me go get a tissue from the bathroom."

"Would you like me to get it for you?"

"No. I can do it."

As Claire left the room, Pricilla glanced at the steamy book cover on the bed. While she hadn't read the romance novel, she was quite certain Claire's tears stemmed from her current situation and not her choice of reading material.

Scooting a chair a few inches away from the wall, she took a seat and adjusted her bifocals. What would Lilian Jackson Braun's fictional detective Qwilleran have done in a situation like this? No doubt he would turn to his crime-sniffing cats Koko and Yum Yum to find the answers. Unfortunately, her own feline friend, Penelope, had never portrayed such high levels of intelligence. Penelope preferred sleeping under a bed or other tight quarters. Still, pet P.I. or not, a good detective could find things that other people would miss.

She slowly took in the details of the room, trying to imprint the image in her mind. A seasoned investigator would notice the pair of women's shoes laying by the fireplace, covered with smudges of mud on the heel, the generic bottles of vitamins, the makeup and jewelry sitting on the dresser, and Charles's open suitcase on the floor.

Concentrating, she pressed her lips together. Among Claire's possessions, there had to be some clue of who hated Charles enough to kill him. No murderer could perform his deadly deed without leaving behind evidence.

"Sorry." Claire walked back into the bedroom with a fistful of tissues and wearing a dark shade of red lipstick that made her pretty face look even paler. "Nothing prepares you for something like this, does it?"

"No." Pricilla thought back to her own experience of losing her husband unexpectedly. "How are you doing today?"

"I don't know." Claire stopped at the picture window that looked out over the mountains toward the north. "I don't know what I'm going to do now. Our marriage wasn't perfect, but it was what I knew. I haven't been on my own since. . .well, I've never been on my own."

"I know how you feel. I lost my husband almost three years ago. We married right out of college."

Frowning, Claire walked to the bed and plopped down on it before picking up a piece of bread and nibbling on the corner. "How did he die?"

"Marty was out playing golf and collapsed on the green with a heart attack."

"So he died doing something he loved."

Pricilla nodded. "After he retired, he golfed at least once a week. It was strange. I almost always joined him except that one Saturday."

Claire's expression softened. "So you weren't there when he died."

Pricilla closed her eyes as the vivid memories returned. "By the time I got to the hospital it was too late."

"I'm sorry." Claire crossed her legs. "And now? Does it get any better?"

"The pain will ease, though I don't know if it ever goes away completely. We'd just celebrated our forty-third anniversary. You can't be married to someone for that long without it taking time to get used to being alone again."

Pricilla stopped. She hadn't come to talk about her

own loss. If Claire was going to heal, she needed to find a way to release the uncomfortable flood of emotions she had to be experiencing. "Tell me about Charles."

A shadow crossed Claire's face. "We'd been married almost twenty years. Doesn't seem long compared to the number of years you spent with your husband, but we did have a good marriage. He was always bringing me flowers and presents."

Claire's claim surprised Pricilla. Not that she had any reason to doubt the woman, but even she had heard Charles and Claire's vicious argument the day they checked in. Not a sign of a marriage gone bad perhaps, but from her own observations, she couldn't help but wonder if Claire was hiding something.

Or perhaps Pricilla was being too critical. Marriages today were difficult to sustain and no one escaped without an occasional rift. The fact that Claire and Charles had stayed together twenty years and beaten the statistics that would have had them divorced years ago had to be evidence that they were doing something right.

Claire dug her fingers into the fabric of the comforter. "Most people didn't know Charles the way I did. They saw him as a ruthless businessman. No one understood how great the pressure was on him. He had a lot to live up to. His father's expectations, for one, in running the family business, and he always had his hand in a number of other projects."

"I understood he had some business contacts with

the other men staying at the lodge this week. Anthony Mills and Simon Wheeler?" Pricilla decided to take the opportunities as they came.

"Really? I wouldn't know. For the most part I stayed out of all his business dealings, though I think it had something to do with a lawsuit he'd recently filed regarding a takeover." Claire shrugged. "We entertained his clients from time to time, but he preferred to meet them at the office or an expensive restaurant. He told me that all his hard work kept him feeling young. In reality, it kept him running, but he loved it. He even planned to go into politics. Said I would make the perfect governor's wife."

Pricilla filed away the new information as Claire spoke about her husband. Perhaps the shock of his death hadn't yet completely worn off. It was after the funeral was over and after everyone had gone home that Pricilla had found handling Marty's death the most difficult. At times, the business of widowhood had completely overwhelmed her. So many details that had to be taken care of. So many daily reminders of what she'd lost.

Pricilla leaned forward, not wanting their conversation to end yet. "And what did you think about the idea of becoming a governor's wife?"

Claire seemed to consider the question. "I was always right there on Charles's arm when he needed me. He always told me that he would take me places with him, and not just physical destinations like Europe and the Caribbean which we frequently traveled through, as well. He was determined to make it socially."

"Where did you come from?"

Claire's laugh seemed to be laced with a hint of bitterness. "A wealthy section of Chicago. Left when I was sixteen. Thought I could make a go of it in Hollywood as an actress. Apparently I didn't have that certain charisma it takes for one to make it past the first round of auditions. I modeled a bit but never landed anything big. That was probably why I always had a hard time believing that Charles would pick me from the dozens of other girls who would have married him in a second. Of course, my parents believed he wanted to marry me for my money, but I knew that wasn't true."

Once again, Pricilla wished she could pull out her notebook and jot down a few comments. Not that her memory was unreliable, but writing had always helped her to solidify things in her mind. Thankfully, while she couldn't run an investigation in the open like Detective Carter could, she was still getting an interesting picture of Claire and her relationship with Charles.

"What was it that drew you to him?" Pricilla asked.

"The first time we met it was his eyes. I'd just left an audition. It hadn't gone well, and I needed to take a walk and compose myself. I ran into Charles—literally—on the corner of West Sunset Boulevard and Whitley Avenue. We stood on the curb for twenty minutes or so, just talking. Didn't take us long to find out that we were both from Chicago and had a lot in common.

"He invited me to lunch, and while it wasn't something I normally did with a complete stranger, I couldn't help but say yes. And the whole time I couldn't keep my eyes off of him. He was tall and handsome, with eyes the color of sapphires. Strong and intense."

Either Claire really had loved her husband and had nothing to do with his murder, or she was putting on a good front. Or maybe she was just lost in the past. A past that was perhaps full of happier memories than the present. That was something Pricilla was determined to find out. For somewhere along the line, Charles had changed from a dashing Casanova to a hardnosed businessman. Hadn't Claire changed as well?

As Claire talked about their first few years of marriage and their struggle to have children, Pricilla forced herself to simply listen to Claire talk without any interruptions. She knew it was necessary to get the most out of their chat. Even if she didn't discover any leads for the case, at least she'd now have an insight into the Woodruffs' life.

After a few minutes, Claire took a deep breath, pausing from her monologue. "It's hard to believe he's dead. I have the money to do anything I want, but the things I once thought were so important don't seem to matter anymore."

Pricilla nodded. All the money in the world couldn't take away the pain of losing a spouse. She knew that.

But there was something else niggling at Pricilla's mind as well. What the woman needed now was something that could only be found in a relationship with Christ. "You said you'd given up your faith when you met Charles. Does that mean you don't believe in God?"

"I did once." Claire shrugged and avoided Pricilla's gaze.

"And now?"

"I can't even tell you when I stopped believing. I stopped feeling God's presence, and He certainly hasn't been there for me lately."

Pricilla didn't miss the bitterness that once again edged Claire's voice, but she knew firsthand that there was only one way to find peace and assurance in such a terrible loss.

Please help me to show her You, Lord.

Pricilla worked to choose her words carefully. "I've lived a lot of years, and I'm still learning how to rely on Christ as my Savior. There's a verse in the Bible that talks about taking refuge in the shadow of God's wing until the disaster has past. I'm convinced a relationship with Christ is the only way to truly find peace in the midst of pain. Our own strength is never enough."

Claire held up her hand. "But don't you see? This is never going to end. Charles is dead, and I have to pick up the pieces. If God were really in control, He would have stopped all of this from ever happening."

"Why?" Pricilla shook her head. "Just because things go wrong in our life isn't proof that God's goodness is any less. Unfortunately the bad choices people make are what lead to sin's consequences. Not God's choices."

Claire's eyes darkened, and Pricilla knew she had pushed the conversation too far for the moment. Claire moved to stand up and knocked over a bottle of vitamins, jumping up as the small tablets scattered across the carpet.

Pricilla stood up as well. "Let me help you pick them up."

The woman glanced up at her, and Pricilla tried to decipher the look of fear in her expression. "No, please. I just need to be alone. I'm sorry. . . ."

Claire knelt down on the carpet and began picking up the small pills.

Not knowing what else to do, Pricilla left the room, wondering exactly what it was she'd just seen in the woman's eyes.

11

Pricilla found Max sitting on the porch, dozing with a book in his hand and Penelope purring on his lap. At least his choice of reading material was better than Claire's, though she herself preferred a good cozy mystery over Max's science fiction books any day. She did wonder, however, if perhaps after this week's events, her reading choices would change to something a little less. . .deadly.

He opened his eyes as she sat down beside him.

"How did it go?" he asked, stifling a yawn.

She pulled out her notebook, not sure what she should write down first. "I learned more about Claire and Charles. According to her, they had a great marriage and were climbing the social ladder straight into politics."

"Interesting." Max rubbed Penelope behind her ears. Both of them still looked half asleep. "Is Claire still at the top of your suspect list after your interview?"

She paused at his question, unsure of the answer. On one hand, it was easy to sympathize with the woman and disregard any suspicions that she might have been involved in her husband's demise. She appeared to have cared about Charles, and did seem to be mourning over her loss. On the other hand, Claire had both motive and opportunity and could easily be covering up any animosity she'd held against her husband.

"I think it's still possible she's hiding something, but someone—or rather two someones—have just moved up on my list."

"Who's that?"

"Anthony and Simon." Pricilla tapped her pen against her paper, certain she was onto something. "Apparently, not only was there a takeover but, according to Claire, a lawsuit as well."

Max's brow rose. "This continues to get more and more interesting."

"You mentioned doing an Internet search on the computer." She dropped the pen and paper onto her lap, praying that they were finally making a step in the right direction. "Could you find specific information on this lawsuit Charles evidently brought against the two men?"

"If the files are public record, it should be fairly easy to find, I suppose." Max rubbed his chin and nodded. "Their motivation for murder is certainly growing. If they made a fortune off a dot-com business and later lost their investments to Charles, they'd have plenty of reason to hate the man."

She knew he was right, but she also couldn't forget her conversation with Claire. "There is something else bothering me, though it doesn't have to do with our suspect list per se."

"What's that?"

Pricilla started doodling a flower on the corner of the open notebook. "Claire asked me why God didn't stop Charles from dying. In other words, if God was in control, why did He let something like this happen?"

"Ah! The age-old question of man. How could a good God let bad things happen?" Max patted his propped up foot and smiled. "And your answer?"

"I told her that things going wrong in our lives weren't proof that God's goodness is any less. Man's bad choices are what lead to sin's consequences."

He nodded. "Good answer."

Pricilla wasn't so sure. "If it was such a great answer then why did she practically kick me out of the room after that?"

"You must have touched a nerve."

She considered his words. Besides physical clues of a crime, there had to be emotional clues as well. Changes in behavior. Uncharacteristic reactions. Had Claire's reaction been one of guilt to a crime, or was it simply that she regretted the fact she'd turned her back on God?

The problem was Pricilla had nothing to compare with what she saw in Claire's behavior today. If she didn't know how the woman normally acted, how could she make an accurate judgment on how she'd conducted herself today? Pricilla had spent little time with either of the Woodruffs before Charles's death. All she had were comments from Nathan and the others who had seen little good in the man.

There was truth in the saying that there is always more than one side to every story. What if Charles had simply been misunderstood? She let out a deep sigh. That didn't change the fact that someone had hated him enough to murder him.

Pricilla added some squiggly lines to her drawing. "No matter what the truth, I can't help but feel sorry for Claire. She seems so lost. They never were able to have children, so she really is alone."

"It's sad to see someone as attractive as she is drawn to the wrong things for fulfillment. Charles had money, but that didn't bring them happiness in the end."

"True, but there's another thing that bothers me about our conversation. She portrayed Charles like a charming Romeo, which is not at all the way everyone else saw him." She set the pencil in her lap and caught Max's gaze. "Granted, I didn't really know the man, but it's obvious Nathan didn't like him, not to mention Simon and his friends. And then there was the rift between him and Oscar."

"Now that's interesting."

"And also a bit odd when you start noticing that practically everyone here had a bone to pick with the man."

"Except his wife."

"Exactly. Which is one reason I can't help but think that she's hiding something."

"Like what?"

Pricilla shook her head, wishing she had the answers. "I don't know yet, but the woman portrayed Charles as too perfect. You know how much I loved Marty, but I'd also be the first to admit that he wasn't perfect. And the same is true for any other couple, I'd think. From everyone that I've talked to, Charles simply wasn't a likable man. He couldn't have been that different in his marriage."

Max folded his hands in his lap. "I see what you're saying, but I still think you're grabbing at straws, Pricilla."

She frowned. Maybe she was. In any case, she didn't seem to be making progress toward the truth, which made her all the more determined to go a step further. "I'm going to go interview Oscar now."

"Pricilla—"

She stood up and made sure to add a measure of determination to her voice. "You can come with me if you'd like, but I plan on talking with him."

Hobbling down the path toward the barn, Max listened to Pricilla vocalize her theories regarding the case while he made sure one of his crutches didn't hit a hole and land him flat on his back again. The last thing he needed right now was another fall. Someone had to watch out for Pricilla, and at the moment, he wanted that someone to be him.

While he normally preferred the warmer winters of New Mexico, he had to admit today was beautiful. The harsh Colorado cold he'd wanted to avoid hadn't yet hit this part of the state, allowing him to enjoy the last of the golden foliage that surrounded them.

"At least something's going right." Pricilla stopped beside a group of white-barked aspen trees and waited for him to catch up with her.

"What's that?" he asked, wondering if he'd missed something she'd said.

"Our children. How do you think Trisha is faring?"

He smiled at the image of his daughter standing on the edge of the lake, reeling in a plump catch. "In the capable hands of your son? I'm sure she's having the time of her life. They seem perfect for each other."

Max glanced at Pricilla out of the corner of his eye. The brisk mountain air had brought out the color in her lined complexion, giving her cheeks a rosy glow—and causing his heart to palpitate. What he really had wanted to say was that the two of them might be perfect together, but after so many years of friendship, he was finding it difficult to figure out a way to change things between them. He didn't want to do anything to ruin their friendship. Maybe they could find a way to start slowly.

Like dating?

The unexpected thought made him want to chuckle. Dating in college had been one thing, but how did one start over forty years later in the courting game? Dinner and a movie seemed too cliché. Sports like rollerblading and bicycling were out of the question, especially with his injured foot. Playing board games around the fireplace might be nice, but would Pricilla think an evening of Scrabble and PBS too dull?

With the Rocky Mountains surrounding them, he followed the winding dirt path beside her, wondering how life had suddenly become so complicated. The whole dating idea seemed ridiculous, which made him wonder if he wasn't looking at the situation in the wrong light. Who said that courtship had to be formal, especially among two friends who had known each other half their lifetimes?

There was another issue that would have to be addressed, as well. While his heart might feel as if he were twenty-five again, the reality was that he was living in a sixty-five-year-old body, and both he and Pricilla were set in their ways. While he didn't like the idea of a long-distance relationship, in order for something to develop between them they would both have to make changes. Moving to Colorado had never been a part of his game plan, and he was certain that Pricilla would have the same reservations about moving to New Mexico and away from her son.

Maybe finding love a second time around wasn't going to be as easy as he'd hoped.

Shoving aside his jumbled feelings for the moment, he stopped beside her a few yards away from the entrance of the barn, sure that the two-story structure was the dream of any rancher. Surrounded by pine and aspen trees, the building's solid timber walls fit perfectly into the mountain scenery.

He glanced at Pricilla, surprised she didn't have

her notebook and pencil out, though he supposed this was a covert operation. "So what's our plan this time? I noticed that you're not carrying a picnic basket full of your cooking."

Her serious expression didn't waver. "I did consider the idea, but thought that might be going a bit overboard."

Max stopped himself from laughing out loud. Since when did Pricilla worry about going overboard? "So any alternative plans?"

"I guess we'll play it by ear. My plans haven't worked so far. I'm hoping to shake my first impressions of the man that weren't good. Maybe that will change if I talk to him for a while."

Somehow Max had his doubts that Oscar would pour on the charm at their arrival. Once Max's eyes adjusted to the dimness of the barn after the bright sunlight, he found his assumptions to be correct. It didn't take words to know that Oscar wasn't happy about the delay in the hunting trip. His sour expression said it all. He stood along one wall of the barn, his broad frame bent over a hunting rifle. Except for the tattoo on his left arm, the guide reminded Max of one of his old military buddies. Rock solid and built like a mountain man.

"Afternoon, Oscar." Pricilla's chipper voice rang out as they walked past the man's pickup and crossed the cement floor of the barn.

The guide glanced at them briefly before shoving

a bronze cleaning brush into the bore of the rifle. "Afternoon."

Max studied the number of high-quality hunting rifles lining the wall and smiled. While he would have preferred not to be a part of Pricilla's wild goose chase to find the murderer, at least he'd found an item of common ground. It looked as if Pricilla wouldn't need any of her lemon crumb cake to get Oscar to talk after all. While her endeavors to coax her suspects to confess were original, he was quite certain that she was out of her league with Oscar. She might know how to whip up an irresistible four-course meal, but he knew his weapons.

He stopped beside Oscar and nodded his approval. "A Winchester M70. Nice firearm. Basic but very accurate. One of the best bolt-action rifles, three-position safety—"

"You sound pretty familiar with your weapons." Oscar took the rifle out of the gun vise and handed it to Max.

Max ran his fingers along the silky walnut stock. He didn't have to pretend to be interested in firearms. "After thirty plus years in the military, I learned a thing or two."

"This one's the Featherweight model and has the standard recoil pad." Oscar folded his arms across his chest. "I use it mainly for beginning hunters, though personally I've always liked its feel and accuracy."

"Max is being far too modest when he says he knows a thing or two." Pricilla took a step back, her smile forced.

He'd forgotten she'd always been skittish around guns. "Max was a small-arms expert in the air force."

"That's impressive." Oscar took the rifle back and took aim at an undisclosed target on the other side of the barn. He pulled on the trigger. "Bang."

Pricilla put her hand over her heart.

"Don't worry." Oscar chuckled as he laid the rifle back in the vise. "I'm in the middle of cleaning it. It's not loaded."

As amusing as Oscar's simulation had been, Max couldn't blame her reaction. With the rifle in the guide's hands, Max certainly didn't want to be the one to discover Oscar was the murderer. He'd prefer Oscar to be friend rather than foe any day.

Oscar leaned against the workbench, his brow raised in question. "So did the two of you need something?"

Apparently, Show and Tell was over. Max looked to Pricilla to answer the guide's question.

"Nothing in particular," she said. "I think we're all feeling cooped up after the hunting trip was canceled."

Oscar sprayed cleaning solvent on the brush he'd used a few minutes ago. "Believe me, that's not all I'm feeling. Can't believe that bald-headed detective had the gall to cancel."

"Still, it's a tragedy about Charles Woodruff, don't you think?" Pricilla wet her lips. "You must have known him fairly well after spending a number of hunting seasons with him."

"Not by choice. It was my job." Oscar's frown deepened, and Max wondered if Pricilla's line of question was too direct. Subtlety took skill.

"I could have done without him on those trips. Never thought he treated folks well, especially Mrs. Woodruff."

"Strange." Pricilla cocked her head. "Claire told me that she and her husband had a good relationship."

"Things are rarely the way they appear. You should know that." Oscar set down the spray can and looked Pricilla in the eye. "You're not out to catch the murderer, now are you, Mrs. Crumb?"

Pricilla held his gaze without flinching. "I believe that's Detective Carter's job."

Max noted the heated glances that passed between Oscar and Pricilla and decided it was time to cut the interview short. "My foot's throbbing, and I need to go and rest my leg, Pricilla. If you're ready to walk back to the house, I think I've had enough exercise for the day."

"I. . .of course." She glanced at him, looking distracted. "Thanks for the demonstration, Oscar. If you'll excuse us—"

Pricilla followed Max back toward the house, feeling as if the questioning had all been in vain. The only new thing she'd learned was the fact that Oscar believed Charles hadn't treated Claire the way he should have.

That discovery, though, didn't surprise her at all.

She tried to organize her thoughts as she and Max made their way up the dirt path and across the gravel driveway. There was another thing that was bothering her. "I suppose if Oscar was the murderer he'd have used the gun he was cleaning rather than poison."

Max shrugged. "It does seem that a bullet in the back of the head would be more his style. Besides, poison's normally connected to women's crimes more so than to men's."

Which led them back to Claire. Or simply in circles. She wasn't sure which.

Pricilla stomped up the porch steps, trying to get the mud off her shoes. "The only common denominator I can find is that no one seemed fond of Charles. But that's not a reason to kill a man."

"We're obviously missing something. Let's examine it more closely." Max sat down in his chair and propped up his foot. "Why do people take the life of someone else?"

She plopped down beside him and mulled over the question. "There could be any number of reasons. Jealousy, murder, blackmail, infidelity, lust. . .the list could go on and on."

"Exactly." He rested his elbows against the arms of the chair. "Anything, in fact, that's in line with the sinful nature."

The thought sent a shiver up her spine. She'd told Claire that humanity's bad choices were what led to sin's consequences. This was true both in the physical sense, as with Charles's death, and in the spiritual sense. Hadn't Paul spoken in Galatians on how the acts of the sinful nature led to death? Murder sounded vile and contemptible, but she'd always been struck by the sins Paul listed.

"What are you thinking?" Max broke into her thoughts.

"I'm thinking how thankful I am for Christ's sacrifice and His forgiveness. It's what the murderer needs. . .what Claire is searching for." She gazed out toward the jagged mountains. "When Paul lists the acts of the sinful nature, he adds things like discord, jealousy, and selfish ambition—things we've all had to deal with—alongside sexual immorality and debauchery. Simply put, we've all sinned. If it wasn't for Christ's death, we'd all be held accountable."

"It's a stark reminder of just how much He loved us, isn't it?"

A shriek of laughter pulled Pricilla away from her somber thoughts. Trisha and Nathan staggered up the drive like a couple of teenagers. Pricilla adjusted her bifocals. If she didn't know better, she'd have thought they were both plastered.

Nathan had his arm around Trisha, whose oversized sweatshirt and jeans were drenched.

Pricilla scooted Penelope off her lap and scurried to the railing. "What in the world happened?"

"Would you believe I fell in the lake?" Trisha's

giggle filled air as she shoved a strand of wet hair from her forehead. "Nathan had to pull me out."

Apparently, Trisha had been Nathan's only catch for the day, but from the look on his face he hadn't minded at all.

Pricilla's motherly instincts took over. "You need to get upstairs, Trisha, and into some warm clothes before you catch your death from pneumonia."

"I know." Trisha laughed. "Thanks, Nathan, for a wonderful time." She laughed again and slopped up the porch steps.

The young woman's cheeks were flushed as Pricilla hurried beside her up the stairs, leaving Pricilla to wonder if the reaction was from the cold or from Trisha's obvious growing feelings toward Nathan.

Pricilla followed Trisha into the Santa Fe room with a stack of towels she'd grabbed out of the upstairs hall closet.

"My friends back home are never going to believe I went fishing, let alone that I fell into the lake." Trisha shivered as she crossed the threshold, but it didn't stop her laughter from ringing out. "Fishing has never been on my to-do list, but I have to say, I had so much fun with Nathan today."

Pricilla couldn't help but echo Trisha's laugh. "Right now, the only thing on your to-do list is to get into some dry clothes."

The drapes that framed the large picture window were open, letting in the last of the afternoon light and some warmth. The sun had begun its descent toward the crest of the mountain range. Once it dropped behind the jagged skyline the temperature would begin to drop as well. Obviously, though, any thoughts of an approaching cold front, or the fact that she was drenched from head to toe, were far from the young woman's mind. One didn't need a degree in psychology to see that the chances of Nathan and Trisha's relationship becoming a lasting one were rising.

And Pricilla couldn't be happier.

She handed Trisha the towels and scurried her into the bathroom. "Would you like me to light the fire before I go?"

Trisha nodded. "That would be wonderful. If you don't mind waiting, I'll be out in just a minute."

Pricilla smiled at the young woman's unbridled enthusiasm, remembering the day she first met Marty. She'd gone home that night and told her roommate she'd just met the man she was going to marry. Love at first sight might seem unbelievable to some people, but she knew it was possible. It might be a while before Trisha and Nathan knew how deep their feelings for each other were, but the beginning seeds of a relationship were already there.

Stopping in front of the stone fireplace, she pulled the box of matches off the mantle. She'd chosen this room for Trisha. Instead of the hunting theme that most of the rooms had, this suite had a Spanish décor with an iron headboard for the bed and matching vanity. The red and green plaids, solids, and floral fabrics of the quilt were picked up in the curtains and throw pillows, giving the room a cozy feel.

Trisha was more than likely used to more modern furnishings, and certainly more modern conveniences than the lodge offered, but despite the fact she was a city girl, the glow in her cheeks was proof that a bit of sunshine, fishing. . .and romance. . .were the perfect prescription for any overworked corporate employee's life.

Pricilla struck a match and moved the yellow flame beneath the pile of kindling in the fireplace. The fire flickered for a few moments, almost dying out, then began to lick the fuel, spreading its fingers around the logs.

A few minutes later, Trisha stepped out of the bathroom, dressed in wool slacks and a long-sleeved top.

"That was quick." Pricilla threw the used match into the fire. "Do you feel better?"

"Definitely warmer. Thank you." Trisha rubbed the ends of her hair with one of the towels. "I need to finish getting ready, but I was wondering. . .would you mind talking for a few minutes?"

"Of course not."

Trisha hung up the towel on the back of the bathroom door then grabbed a black sweater off the vanity chair and slid the sweater on. "My mom and I were always close. I miss having a motherly figure in my life. Especially when it comes to issues of the heart."

Like falling in love?

Trisha grabbed her makeup bag off her bed, stubbing her toe as she rounded the corner. "Akk. . ."

Even a bumped foot couldn't erase the glow on Trisha's face. She sat down at the mirror and unzipped the bag before reapplying her makeup, the smile never leaving her lips. "I suppose it could be a bit awkward for me to talk to you about Nathan. I mean, he is your son. I just feel comfortable around you."

"I don't mind at all." Pricilla leaned forward in the chair she'd chosen for the talk. "So, what do you think about Nathan?"

The question was too forward, but Pricilla couldn't help it. She wanted to know the answer.

Trisha's brow furrowed as she set down her brush, and Pricilla wondered if she had indeed overstepped her boundaries.

"I'm sorry. If my question was too personal—"

"No." Trisha held up her hand. "It's just that I feel guilty, like I should be in mourning instead of out fishing. I mean, the past couple days have been so weird. With Mr. Woodruff's death and all. Honestly, the whole situation's been more than a little bit frightening."

"I certainly agree with you on that point."

Trisha turned toward Pricilla. "But I can't deny the attraction I feel toward Nathan. He's different from anyone else I've ever met."

Pricilla opened her mouth to make a comment then forced herself to shut it. If she wanted Trisha to open up in front of her, she was going to have to give her the opportunity.

"The thing is," Trisha continued as she applied her mascara, "I've had plenty of dates, but this is the first time that I've ever considered giving someone a chance—which surprises me. I've always thought I was too set in my ways and too strong willed for a relationship to really work. Marriage and family have always been out there in the future, but up until now I've never met anyone who makes my heart thud or makes me laugh."

"And now?"

The smile was back on Trisha's face. "I don't know how to describe it, but Nathan brings out something inside me I've never felt before."

"I'm so happy for you. For both of you." Pricilla

reached and gave Trisha a hug. She understood the need to share her life with someone. It was interesting how similar their situations seemed. At least on the surface. She'd thought from time to time how nice it would be to remarry. To let someone into her life who would eat supper with her, share the household responsibilities, and help fill the lonely nights. She missed the companionship of marriage. Wouldn't someone like Max do exactly that?

The question caught her off guard, and suddenly the room began to feel warm. While she'd entertained the thought of remarriage, there was another side to the coin. She enjoyed the freedom to make her own decisions and wasn't sure if she were ready to give that up. And besides, it wasn't as if Max had feelings for her beyond friendship.

Pricilla told Trisha she'd see her at dinner then closed the door to the room behind her. Trisha had mentioned Mr. Woodruff's death, reminding her again that his demise had set her on edge and had her doing things she wouldn't normally do. Not only did they all want to know who had killed the man, she couldn't shake the underlying fear that someone else might be next on the murderer's list. And then there had been her ridiculous feelings of jealousy toward Misty of all people. Something totally out of character for her.

No. Nathan and Trisha had a chance to find true love with each other, but she and Max were a totally different story. They were too good of friends and too set in their ways to think about a relationship.

With her temples throbbing like a jackhammer, Pricilla poured herself a glass of water from the kitchen tap and swallowed two aspirin. Talking with Trisha had been pleasant, but dinner had been a strained ordeal. At least everyone's appetite seemed fine as there had been little of the marinated barbeque meat or salads left, but there hadn't been much conversation during the meal, as everyone seemed to be lost in his or her own thoughts.

She needed to get her mind off the particulars of the case, but was finding it impossible to do so. Her visits with both Claire and Oscar had forced her to realize that there was more involved in the case than she, for now anyway, had been able to work out. Nothing added up. Her fingers drummed against the notebook in her pocket as she tried to force the pieces of the puzzle to fit into something that made sense.

Drawing in a deep breath, she made a mental list for tomorrow's breakfast. The sausage casserole was in the refrigerator along with the fruit salad Misty had made before dinner. There would be little to do tomorrow. . .except prepare meals and try to fill in the missing holes in her investigation. Why was it, though, that nothing she had done so far had brought her any closer to the truth?

She turned off the kitchen light and headed for the living room, her mind trying to wrap itself around the problem. All of the guests, who were also prime suspects according to Detective Carter, were gathered in the spacious room, trying to whittle away the last hours of the evening and add some sense of normalcy to the tense circumstances. Only Claire had decided to go straight to her room after dinner.

Snow had begun to fall outside. Even standing beside the roaring fire did little to take the chill out of the air. Everyone was ready for the murderer to be caught—and the sooner the better.

The grandfather clock in the corner chimed eight. While bits of laughter floated across the room from time to time, it was obvious that everyone was on edge. Despite the detective's order, he could only hold them at the lodge for so long. No one liked the idea that they were confined with a killer on the loose—maybe even among them right now.

Simon and his friends were engaged in a friendly round of poker at the far end of the room. Max and Trisha sat across the room playing a game of Risk. Pricilla had forgotten how much he liked board games and wondered when the last time was that she'd played. She normally spent her afternoons and evenings in the garden, reading, or on one of her latest hobbies. Tonight, even Max's Thomas Kincade puzzle sounded tempting. Anything to break the tension.

"You look cold. I thought you might like some hot chocolate."

Pricilla looked up at Nathan who stood in front

of her with two steaming mugs in his hands. "It does sound good, actually. Thank you."

"She's beautiful, isn't she?"

Pricilla followed his gaze, stopping at Trisha. "Definitely your best choice yet. Why aren't you over there playing with them?"

"I just got here myself. Had a bunch of paperwork to finish up before tomorrow. What do you think about her?"

She took a sip of her drink. "She's smart, pretty, a hard worker. . . . I think you need to hold on to her."

"I think so, too."

Pricilla smiled at her son's comment. She'd expected to have to come up with a lot more scheming with her matchmaking plans, but it was turning out that she didn't have to do anything. Sometimes, love took on a life of its own.

Nathan held the mug between his hands, his gaze focused on the other side of the room. "I know it's not possible, but I don't want her to leave after this week."

"Have you guys talked about a possible future together?"

"It's all happened so quick. I don't want to come across too strong. At least I still have a few days left before she and her father leave."

Pricilla frowned at the thought. Of course, Max would be leaving, too. The idea shouldn't surprise her, but it did. She'd enjoyed their time together these past few days, and while she knew now that her supposed feelings of jealousy were nothing more than the results of stress, one thing was clear. His going back to New Mexico was going to leave an empty space right in the middle of her heart.

~

Max rolled the dice then smiled in triumph as he won against two of Trisha's armies in the Ukraine. "Could it be that your old man just might have the lead in the game for once?"

"The game is far from over, and I'm about to conquer South America." Trisha laughed then leaned forward and caught his gaze. "Honestly, I'm surprised you're making any headway through all of this."

His brows rose in question. "Why would you say that?"

"You've spent the past fifteen minutes continuously glancing at Pricilla."

He leaned back and folded his arms across his chest. "I could say the same for you."

Her attempts to convey an innocent expression didn't fool him at all.

"What do you mean?"

"What do I mean?" He nodded his head toward the fireplace where Pricilla and Nathan stood talking and drinking hot chocolate. "You're only losing because you can't keep your eyes off Nathan."

"That's not true—"

"Isn't it?"

Trisha frowned, but he didn't miss the sparkle in her eyes. "And I thought a nice dueling game of Risk would be a great father-daughter activity tonight, considering everything that's happened."

His smile widened. "It is. I'm enjoying every minute of it."

She handed him one of the dice then rolled her two across the board, wincing at the snake eyes that looked up at her. "Face it, Dad. You'd rather be with Pricilla—"

"And you'd rather be with Nathan."

Max laughed. Falling in love was a complicated thing. He'd never expect both him and Trisha to have their hearts taken at the same time.

He rolled again, beating her last army on Australia. "What do you like about him?"

She groaned and tossed him the dice, her face flushed with a rosy blush. "He's so different from the guys I meet. They're focused on getting ahead in their careers. If they find time for a family, good, but it's not a priority. Nathan's business is important to him, but he also likes to fish and hunt, and he's already showed me that there's more to life than work, something I tend to be a bit obsessed with." She shook her head. "It all seems so fast. . .so out of control even. I mean, I've only known him a few days, yet part of me feels like I've known him forever."

Max rested his elbows on the table. "It's funny. I've

known Pricilla forever, and I'm just now realizing that I want more from our relationship."

"Do you believe in love at first sight?"

He had to consider the question. "I don't know that I've ever thought about it. I first met your mother when she was fourteen years old. One day, I turned around and she'd become a woman. That was the moment I knew I loved her. I was home on leave, and some friends and I were invited to her eighteenth birthday party. She was the one distraction that had me considering going AWOL."

"I'm not surprised at all. Mom was a wonderful woman." Trisha shoved a piece of hair behind her ear. "I never believed in love at first sight. . .until now."

"Then what are you doing?"

"What do you mean?"

Max slapped his hands against the table. "Stay here."

With a new resolve, Max rose from the table and hobbled across the room to where Pricilla and Nathan stood.

"How's the game going?" Nathan asked.

Max caught the longing in the young man's eyes. It was clear he'd rather be sitting at the table with Trisha. "Thought you might want to take my place."

Nathan grinned. "Are you sure? I thought this was a father-daughter evening."

"Who are we kidding? You'd rather be with Trisha, and I'd love to keep Pricilla company." He leaned forward. "By the way, I'm winning, but she's good."

Nathan laughed. "I think I can handle myself. I—"

Misty burst into the room. Pricilla jumped beside Max, dropping her mug. The ceramic slammed against the stone hearth.

"I'm sorry." Misty held her hand against her chest. "But it's Claire. She's missing."

13

Pricilla's hot chocolate seeped across the stone hearth and onto the carpet, but Pricilla couldn't move. She had suspected Claire had something to hide and now she was certain.

Nathan stepped forward. "I want you to take a deep breath, Misty, and calm down."

Everyone's gaze was riveted on the young housekeeper as she took a few deep breaths and tried to relax before she continued talking. "Claire asked me to bring her a cup of tea at eight o'clock, so I made some for her, headed for her room, and knocked on her door. She didn't answer. I thought she might be asleep, but I was worried about the woman. I mean she just lost her husband, and I know how awful it feels to have someone walk out on you, though it wasn't as if Charles did it on purpose, I suppose. I mean—"

Nathan laid his hand on her shoulder. "Why don't you stick to what happened to Claire for now?"

"I'm sorry. You're right. It's just that—never mind." She flipped back a section of her blond hair. "Anyway, I opened Claire's door and saw that she wasn't in her room. I looked in the bathroom and even on the outside balcony, but she wasn't there. That wasn't the most bizarre thing, though. I've been cleaning her room everyday, so I know what should be there. And, well, her purse and most of her clothes are now gone."

Pricilla's eyes widened. She glanced around the room at each of the guests—or *suspects*, as she was sure Detective Carter had officially labeled them all. It was like a scene from one of Agatha Christie's mystery novels. They were all gathered in the parlor, and there was a murderer on the loose. It could be any one of them. And now Claire was missing. And in Pricilla's mind, if she'd run away from the lodge, it could mean only one of two things. Either Claire was the murderer, or she had something to hide.

Pricilla worked to swallow the lump that had risen in her throat. Maybe there was a third possibility? Could the murderer have struck again? She shook her head. Nathan was right. They all needed to calm down. Jumping to conclusions would do nothing but ensure a panic.

She tugged on Nathan's sleeve and pulled him aside. The room was filled with the murmur of voices. As much as Pricilla didn't like Detective Carter and his patronizing methods, even she knew when to draw the line. "We need to call the sheriff."

"Just a minute." He held up his hand and addressed the group. "Before we overreact to the situation, we need to do our own quick search of the lodge. Claire could have gone for a walk, gone out to see the horses in the barn, or any number of things."

Trisha glanced out the window. "Her car's still here. That may mean she hasn't left the property."

Nathan nodded. "See what I mean? More than likely she just stepped out of her room. No use calling the detective unless we have a real crisis to report. Now. Let's all split up to look for her, and meet back here in fifteen minutes."

Misty knelt and began to pick up the shards of broken ceramic. "I'll clean up the mess, Mrs. Crumb. Feel free to go look for Mrs. Woodruff with the others."

Pricilla nodded her thanks and headed for the kitchen. Max hobbled along beside her down the long, narrow hallway. Misty had probably had enough stress for one night, and she couldn't blame the young woman. Pricilla slowed her steps. She'd never noticed how eerie the lodge felt at night. The iron sconces left shadows dancing on the walls. A dog barked in the distance, but beside that there was little noise but the sound of her footsteps and the uneven thump of Max's crutches on the hardwood floor.

"I never knew how exciting life could be with you," Max said, breaking the silence between them. "I'd planned to ask you to join me for a game of Scrabble until this most recent incident occurred."

She laughed. "This is becoming to be too much excitement, if you ask me."

"I agree. I'm too old for games of cloak-and-dagger."

"Except there are no spies involved in this game. Only dead bodies and a lodge full of suspects."

The kitchen light was on, and Oscar was filling a plate with leftovers. He balanced the food and soda in his hands then shut the refrigerator door with his foot. "Hope you don't mind, Mrs. Crumb. One of the horses is a bit colicky tonight, and I've been tied up in the barn until now."

"Of course I don't mind." Pricilla paused at the bar. "Have you seen Mrs. Woodruff? She seems to be missing."

"No." Oscar's brow narrowed. "I haven't seen her at all today, in fact. Is something wrong?"

Max laid his crutches against the counter. "We don't know yet. We're trying to find her."

Oscar pulled out a roll of plastic wrap and covered his plate. "I just came from the barn. Unless I missed her in the dark. . ."

Pricilla shook her head. "I don't suppose there would have been any reason for her to go to the barn, but just in case, would you mind walking there with me once you get your food together? Max can't be on crutches in the dark, and I'd prefer not to go alone."

Oscar shrugged. "I'm ready now."

"Pricilla, I think you should—"

"I'll be fine." She glanced at Max, whose expression told her clearly that he wasn't happy with her plan. "Like Nathan said, she's probably gone for a walk or some other harmless activity. Don't worry."

She grabbed a flashlight from the junk drawer by the stove and stepped out the back door with Oscar before Max could stop her. While she'd far rather be sitting in front of the fireplace, playing a game of Scrabble with Max, she was determined to get to the bottom of things. This new twist in the case had her mind scrambling once again to put the pieces together. What she had, though, wasn't enough to finish the outer edges of even the simplest puzzle.

Pricilla's breath blew out in white puffs in front of her. "It's been a strange week, hasn't it?"

"Yep," Oscar mumbled.

"I've never been involved in a murder investigation."

Oscar grunted, and Pricilla felt a sense of déjà vu. Apparently, like Simon and his buddies, conversations weren't Oscar's forte. How was one supposed to do a thorough investigation when constantly greeted with grunts and one-syllable answers?

She shone the flashlight down the moonlit path, making sure she walked slow enough to avoid the ruts, while at the same time trying to keep up with Oscar's long steps.

Moonlight caught Oscar's rigid jaw line, and she shivered. Taking a deep breath, she reminded herself that the chances of Oscar having anything to do with the murder were slim. He had no known motive except that he, like everyone else, had disliked the dead man. The reason for Charles's dislike of Oscar was still unclear in her mind, but she wasn't convinced it had anything to do with the murder.

She looked up at the aspen trees that swayed in the wind along the path like a group of dancers. The snow had stopped falling, leaving a dusting of white powder that glistened beneath the glow of the moon's light. They were almost halfway to the barn. She decided to make another stab at a conversation.

"Have you always lived in Colorado?"

"Kansas originally."

"Any family?"

The darkness masked his expression this time. "My parents died in a car crash when I was seventeen. My sister still lives in Kansas."

"Is she married?"

"Five years, to a computer geek from Cincinnati."

"And what about you?" She steered the conversation back to him. "Why'd you move to Colorado?"

He let out a breath that clouded the cold air as they neared the barn. "My friends used to spend their breaks skiing in the mountains, but my family could never afford it. Went camping a few times and discovered I liked the outdoors. I may never be able to afford a condo in Breckenridge, but at least I'm here more than one or two weeks out of the year."

She tried to sense bitterness in his words for growing up poor, but if it was there, it didn't show. Besides, the man had a point. Two weeks out of the year wasn't nearly long enough to enjoy the beauty of this area.

The barn was dark except for a lit light bulb at the entrance. Oscar flipped on another light, illuminating the rack of guns on the far wall.

"Mrs. Woodruff?" Pricilla's voice echoed in the large structure. She breathed in the fresh scent of the hay. "Mrs. Woodruff, are you here?"

There was no answer except for the low snort of a horse in one of the stalls.

"I don't think she's here." Oscar set his plate of food down on a long wooden counter.

Pricilla turned to face him. "Did you know her well?"

"Mrs. Woodruff?" He shrugged a shoulder. "Why would I have known her?"

"She stayed at the lodge a number of times. You must have run into her once or twice."

Oscar rubbed his goatee and shook his head. "Of course I saw her around. I just don't normally have a lot of contact with those who don't go hunting, and Mrs. Woodruff never did."

Pricilla paused, wondering if once again she was pushing too hard. Max had warned her that her snooping into the case was going to get her into trouble. With a wall full of hunting rifles and a possible murderer standing in front of her, she hoped this wasn't the time Max proved himself right. She was too far from the house for anyone to hear her scream if he was.

Oscar popped open the tab of his cola.

Pricilla jumped then chided herself for her uneasiness.

He blew on the fizz before taking a sip. "I'll let

you know if I see Mrs. Woodruff, but until then I have dinner to eat and a horse to tend to—"

"Of course." Pricilla took a step backward. "Thanks for letting me walk with you. I'm sure they've already found her by now anyway."

She walked slowly back to the lodge, hoping someone had actually found Claire. While Pricilla wanted the woman to be innocent, Claire did have both motive and opportunity.

Something howled in the distance, sending goose bumps down Pricilla's spine. She pulled her sweater around her, wishing she'd grabbed her heavy coat before coming out here. Max had been right. Once again she'd acted before thinking and would risk the chance of getting sick if she didn't get warm soon.

Her beam caught movement up ahead, and she froze. Another howl broke through the stillness of the night, but this time it was closer. Something was out there. A wolf? A dog? She had her mind set on staying clear of a murderer, not a wild animal that might cross her path.

"Pricilla, it's me."

"Max?" She raised the flashlight and shined the light in his eyes.

"Put that thing down." He reached out and shoved the beam of light back down to the ground.

With her heart racing, she took a deep breath. "What in the world are you doing out here? You don't even have a flashlight."

"It's a full moon and I have two perfectly good

weapons." He held up one of the crutches.

She pressed her hand against her chest. "You about gave me a heart attack."

"What about me?" The combination of the sound of his voice and the light of her flashlight were enough to tell her that he wasn't smiling. "You go tearing off in the dark with a possible murderer without thinking twice about it."

"I—"

"I'm not finished yet. You seem to have forgotten that there's a murderer on the loose. Otherwise you wouldn't have done something as foolish as go out in the dark with one of the suspects. Besides, you really didn't think I was going to let you go off by yourself, did you?"

"What could you have done? You have a sprained foot—" Pricilla bit back the comment. He was right. She hadn't thought. If Oscar had wanted to harm her, there wouldn't have been anything she could have done. Wit and mental power might be handy in a game of Scrabble or Risk, but she would have been no match physically to a thirty-something-year-old male with a rack of rifles on the wall. Who was she fooling?

She shook her head. "Of course, you're right, Max. I'm sorry."

"You should be." The lines around his eyes softened. "You had me worried that something awful was going to happen to you."

"Have they found Claire yet?"

"I don't know. I've been wobbling toward the barn the whole time you were gone."

She couldn't help but chuckle at his comment. "I'm sorry, but it does make a humorous picture. Your running after me in the dark on your crutches. . . I am sorry."

"Just stop taking so many gambles with your life." Did she sense a hint of amusement in his voice? "As much as I am opposed to getting involved with this entire mess, there is something else I found out tonight."

Pricilla stopped. "What is it?"

"I found a few moments to do a bit of digging around on the Internet and came across an interesting interview."

"Yes—?"

Max started back up the path, this time in the light of her flashlight. "After the dot-com business was sold, Michael Smythe took his share of the money and pursued a lifetime dream to become an independent producer of video games. His first game was an immediate success."

She kicked a rock out of the path with the toe of her shoe. "No connection to Charles, though, right?"

"Not yet, but in digging deeper, I discovered that while Michael didn't partner with the two men, he did invest heavily in their endeavor."

The lights of the lodge lit the path and Pricilla turned off her flashlight. "So when Simon and Anthony lost all their money, Michael took a big hit as well."

"A huge loss, apparently."

"Which keeps all three of them on the list of suspects."

Max nodded. "Especially considering the fact that the takeover was not pretty."

At the lodge, Nathan paced across the porch, talking to someone on his cell phone, his fist balled at his side. Trisha leaned against the rail. There was no one else on the porch.

"Have you found her?" Pricilla rushed up the stairs, ignoring the throb in her hip.

Trisha turned and shook her head. "Not unless you found her in the barn."

Nathan flipped the phone shut and joined the three of them.

"Did you call the detective?" Max asked.

"No, the detective called me." Worry lines were etched into his forehead. "He had a follow-up question to our conversation earlier today. I didn't tell him about Claire."

Trisha rested her hand on Nathan's arm. "I think you need to call him back and tell him what's happened."

Nathan's frown deepened. "As much as I don't want to, I suppose I should."

Trisha was right, of course. They would have to call the detective. But that didn't mean she would have to stay up and see him. Surely he wouldn't have the gall to get her out of bed.

"Since there's nothing else I can do, I think I'm

going to head up to bed. We can talk more about what you found out tomorrow."

Max smiled at her. Maybe he'd forgiven her.

He headed into the house behind her. "Chicken."

Or maybe not.

She turned to face him. "Okay. I admit it, Max. I'm avoiding an encounter with the detective."

"Sleep well." He winked at her and headed toward the kitchen. "I'll see you in the morning."

"Good night."

At the end of the upstairs hallway, Pricilla paused at her room. Was it only a few short days ago that she'd looked forward to a quiet week with Max and Trisha? Life had gotten complicated, and quickly. She preferred murder and mysteries to be savored within the pages of a good book—not experienced in real life. Who was she to think she could solve a real life whodunit? Pulling her key from her pocket, she slid it into the lock. Miss Marple had an uncanny intuition. Father Brown had a deepened spiritual insight. She, on the other hand, had—

Pricilla froze. The door wasn't locked. She tried to relax. Undoubtedly she'd simply forgotten to lock it.

Slowly, she pushed the door open. Claire was sitting on her bed.

"I have to tell someone the truth." The woman's stoic expression never wavered as she spoke. "I'm the one who murdered Charles."

14

Pricilla leaned against the doorframe for support. The day had obviously been too tiring for her. Here she was, a sixty-four-year-old woman with bifocals and a girdle, standing in the doorway of her room, listening to a murder confession.

Things like this didn't happen to people like her. They happened to priests, and ministers, and undercover FBI agents.

She took a tentative step forward. Maybe it was time to add a hearing aid to the list. "What did you say?"

"I said I killed Charles."

Pricilla shook her head to try and clear it. "You're confessing to his murder?"

In actuality, Pricilla wasn't so much surprised at the fact that it had actually been Claire who did it but that the woman was confessing to her that she had done it.

Claire raked her fingers through her hair and nodded. "Whoever said that confession was good for the soul was right. I've felt like I was going to be eaten alive by the guilt. I finally couldn't take it anymore."

Pricilla studied Claire's face. Her eyes were red and swollen from crying, but a sense of relief was obvious in her expression as well. Stress did weird things to people. Having one's husband murdered would certainly top her list.

Claire dug into the comforter with her fists. In her jeans and forest green sweater, and painted nails, she looked like a typical hotel guest. Nothing about her stood out. In fact, she looked a bit vulnerable. Certainly not capable of murder. . . Or was she?

Pricilla took a step toward the bed. "Are you sure you're not just overwrought? You've been through a traumatic experience."

"There's nothing wrong with me." She hiccupped. "Well, nothing besides the fact that I will live out the rest of my life in prison."

A shadow crossed Claire's face, and Pricilla wondered if she'd actually thought through the consequences of her actions or if her only goal had been to confess. Something definitely wasn't right. "Have you been drinking?"

Claire shook her head. "I hiccup when I'm nervous."

Pricilla chewed on her bottom lip. Out of all the scenarios she had played through her mind in solving the case, this certainly hadn't been one of them. A clandestine meeting at night in her own room seemed more like something from a B-rated movie than from her own life.

Pricilla sat down on the bed beside her. "Tell me what happened?"

Claire hiccupped again then clinched her hands against her stomach. "I've made so many bad choices, I don't know where to begin."

Max would be furious to know that she was sitting beside a confessed murderer, but at the moment she didn't feel any fear. Only a deep sorrow and pity for the woman. Besides, Claire was obviously in a daze.

"Try starting from the beginning," Pricilla suggested. "It always helps."

Claire took a laborious breath. "I planned it weeks ago after I found out he was cheating on me. I used a slow acting poison from a private source. You wouldn't believe how easy it is to get your hands on something like that. Cost me a fortune, all right, but took little effort. Charles thought the pills were vitamins. Something to help boost his immune system. He worked so many hours and was always tired. He'd take anything I suggested that might give him that extra boost. He never complained when I reminded him every morning to take them. Never suspected a thing."

"Why are you telling me this now? Why confess?"

Claire shrugged. "Besides the fact that I couldn't hold the truth inside a second more, I'm pretty sure the authorities would find out eventually. Once the toxicology report comes in, they'll search my things and find a trail that leads to me. It would be funny if it wasn't so tragic. I couldn't wait for Charles to die. But now that he's gone, I actually regret killing him."

Pricilla tried to picture the woman in a jail cell. Overcrowded conditions. Prison garb. Greasy food. The images were far from pleasant, and Claire certainly wasn't the kind of person one imagined visiting in cellblock D. Sculpted eyebrows, manicured nails, and a bit of plastic surgery and liposuction thrown in along the way. . . Not exactly the poster girl for your local prison population.

Pricilla fought to understand. "Lots of husbands cheat on their wives but that doesn't give their wives the license to kill them. Did he abuse you?"

"Not physically, but there are plenty of other kinds of abuse." She kept her voice calm with barely any inflection. "I never thought it would have driven me to murder either, but my marriage was a farce, far from the perfect situation I tried to show everyone."

Claire got up and walked to the window. Pulling open the heavy drapes, she let the moonlight spill across the bedspread with a forest scene pattern. "Six months ago, I found out that my husband was having an affair with his secretary, and I confronted him."

Pricilla didn't know what to say. She'd informally counseled dozens of people over the years. Young mothers who needed an older woman to talk to. Someone who wouldn't judge, could give advice freely, and most importantly, someone who would just listen. The advice part came easily. She'd worked hard to make sure that she listened as well.

But this was different. She'd heard women pour out their hearts over husbands who'd left them with small children, or who had deserted them after their children had left home. Women who'd lost everything they had because of their husband's indiscretions. But murder was completely out of her league.

"I'm sorry," she said, simply.

Claire ran her fingers down the thick drapes. "I know that I was as much to blame for our problems as he was. It's ironic, really. This trip was supposed to be a chance for us to make things right in our relationship. On the surface, anyway. I knew nothing would ever change between us.

"There were money problems, as well. He would never have divorced me. I have my own money from my father's estate. Divorce would have completely ruined him financially, something he would never have handled. He was content to pretend that all was well with us, another one of his lies."

Pricilla leaned back and rested her hands on the bed. "So what happens now?"

Claire's gaze dropped, and she scuffed the toe of her leather boots against the carpet. Maybe the reality of what she'd done in confessing was starting to sink in. "I suppose the detective will need to be called."

"He should be on his way actually. Misty told us you'd disappeared, and we've all been out looking for you."

"So, I've become a fugitive." Claire laughed, a short hollow laugh. "Can I ask you something?"

"Of course."

Claire came and sat back down on the bed beside Pricilla. "Did you mean it when you said that God was good, and that He was in control?"

"Yes."

"Do you think He could ever make something out of the mess I've made of my life?"

Pricilla closed her eyes and quickly prayed for wisdom. Then she said, "One thing I've been struck with lately is that we've all sinned. Your consequences might be greater right now, but God speaks just as loudly against those who envy and gossip. Something I'm sure we're all guilty of. To God, sin is sin, but He promises us that for those who trust Him and serve Him, He will forgive us our sins and purify us."

"I find that hard to believe. I took a life. . . ." Claire wiped away a tear and sniffled.

"There are tissues in the bathroom," Pricilla suggested.

"Thanks," Claire said vaguely. She walked into the bathroom, shutting the door behind her. Pricilla had a few moments to catch her breath. The window was too small for Claire to crawl through, so she didn't have to worry about the woman escaping.

Claire's confession had Pricilla's mind spinning. How could someone kill her husband? Divorce was extreme enough, but murder was so. . .so final. She pulled off her sweater and threw it on the bed. If Nathan had managed to get a hold of the detective, he could be here any minute. And she was sure that the detective would find pleasure in arresting Claire. He'd have his murderer and the case would be solved. And a case closed would please his uncle. All her harebrained ideas had done nothing to solve the case.

Someone knocked on the door.

She crossed the room to open it.

"Detective Carter!"

"Mrs. Crumb—" The bathroom door opened behind her, and the detective's eyes widened. "And Mrs. Woodruff?"

Pricilla cleared her throat. "I found her."

"I can see that." He pulled off his glasses and waved them at her. "And do you know what the penalty is for harboring a suspect in a murder investigation?"

Did he just accuse her of a crime? "Harboring a suspect? Detective Carter, that's ridiculous. I wasn't harboring anyone. I found Claire in my room. Surely you don't think that I would ever do such a. . .such an illegal thing."

"Don't I?" He slid his glasses back on and caught her gaze.

"It's not her fault." Claire grabbed her purse and squeezed it against her chest as she walked toward the detective. "I was in her room when she came in. Mrs. Crumb didn't have any choice but to listen to me confess—"

"Confess to what?" Claire had the detective's full attention.

The woman held her head up high. "I'm the one who poisoned my husband."

The detective folded his hands across his chest and stood looking at both women for a moment. "Now isn't this an interesting turn of events. Are you willing to come down to the station and make a complete confession?"

"Yes." Claire's voice wavered.

The detective pulled a pair of handcuffs out of his back pocket.

Pricilla stepped between Claire and Detective Carter. "Do you have to handcuff her?"

"As much as I'd like to humor you, Mrs. Crumb, my only goal is to see that justice is served, and in doing that it is my duty to uphold the letter of the law." The detective glanced at Claire as if evaluating his decision. "But I suppose I could make an exception this time."

Pricilla nodded in surprise. It was the first glimpse of humanity she'd seen in the man.

Claire preceded the detective out of the room, a glazed expression across her face. Pricilla looked at the clock. Nine. Just an hour ago she'd been about to play an innocent board game. Now all Pricilla knew how to do was pray.

Three hours later, Pricilla glanced at the digital clock. Again. She couldn't sleep. She threw off the comforter. Maybe she was just hot. The logs in the fireplace no longer burned with their orangish glow, but the room was stuffy. Rolling over, she pushed off the thick comforter and let out a deep breath. She needed to relax, but all she could see was Claire's face as she confessed that she'd murdered her husband.

She turned over the other way, but it was no use. If she took a sleeping pill this late at night, she'd never get up in the morning. A cup of tea was the second best thing.

Flipping on the light beside her bed, she sat up and yawned then wrapped her robe firmly around her. She found her slippers under the bed and padded downstairs to the kitchen. Apparently, she wasn't the only one who couldn't sleep. Trisha sat on one of the bar stools with a mug in one hand and a book in the other.

Pricilla stopped in the doorway. "Can't sleep either?"

Trisha set down the book and shook her head. "Every time I close my eyes, I see the look on Claire's face as the detective carted her off to jail. The whole thing is too weird. I don't understand why she would confess like that. There's got to be something else going on."

"I know what you mean, but what?" Pricilla grabbed a cup and filled it with water before putting it in the microwave. "I have some over-the-counter sleeping pills, if you want to try one."

Trisha lifted up her mug. "I'm trying hot milk, but it's not working."

"Never worked for me either."

With the water heating, Pricilla flipped through the tea canister and debated over what kind she wanted. Avoiding caffeine was a no-brainer. Too much of the stimulant and she wouldn't be able to sleep, even with a pill.

One blend claimed it would relax her so she would

be able to sleep like a baby. It had been years since she'd slept like a baby, but it was worth a try.

"I had a friend who had some interesting remedies for falling asleep." Pricilla leaned against the counter and waited for the water to heat up. "Marjorie was convinced that sleeping with her head facing north guaranteed a good night's sleep. Something to do with the magnetic field of the planet or something."

Trisha took another sip of her milk and grimaced. "My mom always told me to lie in bed and wiggle my toes. It was supposed to relax me."

The microwave beeped and after taking out the mug, Pricilla dropped her tea bag into the hot water. "Maybe I should try both suggestions."

"I suppose it couldn't hurt, though I don't know if Nathan would appreciate my rearranging the furniture to ensure I was lying in the right direction." Trisha got up and dumped the rest of her milk down the drain. "So, you have some magic pills, do you?"

Pricilla chuckled. "When you get to be my age, you can't be without them."

Pulling her plastic pillbox out of the cupboard, she set it down on the counter and noted Trisha's raised brow. "Don't tell me that your father doesn't have one of these stashed away. It's all part of the joys of growing old."

Pricilla ran her finger across the plastic container. From painkillers to blood pressure medicine, herbal vitamins to sleeping pills, she'd managed to organize her daily doses down to a science.

"Now for sleeping pills. These are prescription, so Detective Carter would come after me if I gave them to anyone. These two contain an antihistamine, so you might feel sluggish come morning." Pricilla popped open one of the compartments. "And this one"—she popped open another—"is a dietary supplement that is supposed to help regulate your sleep-wake cycle. You can take your pick."

Trisha tapped one of the pills with the tip of her finger. "Wow. I have a choice? I had no idea there was a selection."

"Believe me, this is only the beginning of what's available." She nudged Trisha with her shoulder. "Personally, I avoid them whenever possible, but my doctor agreed it's all right every now and then, so I like to be prepared. And frankly, I'd say involvement in a murder investigation is a valid reason."

"At least the case is pretty much closed now." Trisha poured a glass of water and took a sip. "How in the world do you keep these straight?"

"Get to be my age and you won't have a problem. Unless, of course, you suffer with memory loss." She caught the worried expression on Trisha's face. "It's really not that bad. I've got an herbal pill for that as well."

Trisha guffawed. "I needed to laugh. Life's become too serious lately."

Pricilla handed her one of the pills. "This is a mild one. Take it and go on up to bed. You can sleep in tomorrow as late as you want."

Trisha grabbed the pill, but Pricilla didn't miss the blush that crept up the young woman's face. "Well, the detective finally said we are all free to come and go as we like. With the men leaving on their hunting trip tomorrow, Nathan's planning to take off a couple of hours so that he can take me out to breakfast in town."

Pricilla beamed inwardly. "I'll make sure you wake up. You'll be missing my peaches and cream French toast, but I have the feeling that neither of you will mind a bit."

"Somehow I have a feeling that you're right." Trisha swallowed the pill with a glass of water then kissed Pricilla on the cheek. "Thank you for everything."

"You're welcome." She'd always wanted a daughter. A daughter-in-law would be just fine. "Sleep tight."

Pricilla took a sip of her tea and watched as Trisha floated out of the kitchen. She needed to finish her drink and try to sleep as well. She'd never make it through tomorrow if she didn't get some rest.

She wondered how Claire was doing right now. At some point, the shock of what had happened was going to wear off. That's when things would get really tough. That's when she would really need a relationship with Christ to get her through. Without it, Pricilla honestly didn't know how people coped with tragedies. She'd keep praying for Claire and maybe even visit her. There was nothing else she could do at this point.

Pricilla started down the hall toward the stairs.

Something niggled at the back of her mind, but she couldn't put a finger on it. Ever since she'd talked to Claire that time in the woman's bedroom, she had felt that something was off. A small detail that didn't add up. Feeling the stiffness in her joints, she took the stairs slowly. Max would tell her that she was overtired and being paranoid, and he was probably right. She was also certain that he was thrilled she was out of the detective business for good. And so was she. . .for the most part. There had been something exciting about planning, trying to phrase the right questions, and putting together the pieces of the puzzle.

But all of that was over now.

Pricilla yawned and tried for the third time to read the recipe out of the cookbook for peaches and cream French toast. Three hours of sleep wasn't enough to keep a snail moving at half speed, and it certainly wasn't enough to keep her eyelids open. Her vision doubled as she tried adjusting her bifocals. Maybe she should serve something simpler this morning—like cold cereal and bananas.

But of course she wouldn't.

Instead she poured herself a cup of coffee—thick and black—and tried to wake up. It wasn't as if she needed as much sleep as she did when she was younger, or that she'd never suffered from sleepless nights before, but there was a minimum amount required to function. She obviously hadn't reached that point.

She flipped the pages of the recipe book and settled on cherry-cinnamon muffins. Fifteen minutes prep time she could handle. Add a few simple side items like yogurt and bacon, and her guests would be happy. There might even be time for a midmorning nap, something she seldom indulged in.

Pricilla paused before pulling out the ingredients for the muffins. Her spiral detective notebook sat beside the recipe book, an empty page staring up at her. She flipped through the slips of paper and frowned.

So much for her lists of suspects, motivations, and interviews. All they had got her was knee deep into a number of embarrassing situations and not one step closer in solving the case.

But life was back to normal now. She no longer had to worry anymore about interrogations, clues. . .or Detective Carter for that matter.

"Good morning." Max's voice rang entirely too chipper from the kitchen doorway.

She turned to face him. "Why the super-sized grin this morning?"

He bridged the gap between them, his crutches thudding against the floor. "Nothing like a good night's sleep after a murder's been solved."

Pricilla groaned. "I take it you weren't up half the night then."

"And you were?"

She pointed to the box of tea on the counter and shook her head. "Let's just say, don't believe the one that claims you'll sleep like a baby after drinking it. Of course, I'm sure they would include murder as an exemption in their ads."

Max folded his arms across his chest and chuckled. "Of all people, I thought you would have slept good last night, knowing the case is solved."

"One would think." She tried to open the jar of sour cherries then handed it to Max.

"It couldn't have ended better to me." He strained, balancing on his good foot, then popped open the jar. "With life back to normal, I can spend the rest of the week with you without your little notebook coming between us."

Pricilla ran her hand down her cheek, suddenly wishing she'd spent more time trying to erase the crow's feet and age spots. "Glad you slept well."

"And why didn't you? You should be relieved."

"I am." Pricilla pulled a glass bowl out of the bottom cupboard then went in search of the measuring cups. "But I don't understand how Claire could have killed her husband. She told me he was unfaithful to her. If you ask me, he should be the one locked up for his indiscretions. Instead, she's going to pay for her decision the rest of her life."

"But isn't that what it comes down to? It was her decision." Max popped one of the sour cherries into his mouth. "Besides, I'm sure there's more to the story than either of us will ever know."

"I suppose, but don't you wonder how God could have allowed the woman to suffer so much pain that she in turn took someone's life?"

Max knitted his brow and appeared to mull over his answer. "I would assume there's got to be a lot of baggage that goes behind a decision like Claire's. You can't blame God for her bad choice."

"Of course, you're right." She measured the flour and dumped it into the bowl. "It's still sad though. Her life will never be the same again, no matter what happens."

"I was wondering. . ." Max cleared his throat and

dropped his gaze for a moment. "I was wondering if you felt like going into town today? I thought I could take you out to lunch. Might be a nice break for you, considering everything that's happened here the past couple of days."

Pricilla smiled. If Misty served lunch, she should be able to enjoy a quiet break with Max. She'd planned a special celebration dinner tonight, but if she left a list of things for Misty to get done, she should have plenty of time to have everything ready by seven.

She watched as Max fidgeted in front of her. Funny how the mention of them going to lunch had him squirming like a seventeen-year-old asking her out to the prom. She shook her head. It must be her imagination. The lack of sleep could do funny things to a person. Besides, it wasn't as if this were a date or anything. They would go to the Rendezvous Bar and Grill, or one of the small town's other restaurants and enjoy the establishment's specials for the day that would be enhanced by engaging conversation.

She felt her heart skip a beat. "Lunch would be perfect."

Twenty minutes later, with the muffins in the oven and Misty setting up the dining room for breakfast, Pricilla headed upstairs. She expected that there would be quite a few smiling faces this morning, but the nagging feeling that something wasn't right continued to pester her. She wanted to know how Claire could have been driven to murder her husband.

Pricilla stopped in front of the Elk Room and hesitated. The detective had already made a search last night and removed all the evidence. What could a bit of snooping on her behalf matter at this point? It wasn't as if she expected to find any more clues. Even she knew that the case would soon be officially closed by the coroner and sheriff's department. There was nothing left for her to discover. But that didn't stop her from wanting to take one last look.

"Mom?"

Pricilla pulled her hand back from the door knob like it was a hot ember. She shoved her hands behind her back. "Nathan, you scared me."

"What are you doing?" He cocked his head, seemingly amused at the fact that he'd caught her red-handed. "In case you forgot, the case is closed."

"I know. I was just. . ." She took a step away from the door, swallowed any feelings of guilt, and decided to change the subject. "Where are you off to this morning? You're looking quite handsome."

He tugged on the collar of his muted green sweater and grinned. "I'm taking Trisha out for breakfast. I'm assuming you approve?"

She smiled and the tension of the moment began to fade. "You know I do, and a date is definitely a step in the right direction."

"As long as it's the first of many."

Pricilla smiled to herself. It was obvious Nathan was smitten. So much, in fact, that the mere thought of

Trisha had him losing his concentration and forgetting the fact that he'd caught his mother about to go into Claire's room to investigate a closed case.

She reached up and brushed off a piece of lint from his shoulder. "I hope it will be the first of many as well."

"Did you see the *Rendezvous Sentinel* this morning? They just announced Charles's death and put a stock photo of the lodge on the front page. They'll be calling today, though, now that Claire has been arrested. I plan to be away from the phone, giving my attention to more important things. Like Trisha." He smiled. "I just wish we had more time before she had to leave."

"A long-distance relationship is always an option for a while." Pricilla tried to ignore the reminder that Max would be leaving in four days, as well.

"I've never believed in a long-distance relationship, but I've decided to talk to her about that this morning. Time's running out and nothing will happen if I don't take a chance."

Life was full of taking chances. Was that what Claire had done? Took a chance that killing her husband would bring her something better in life? That something certainly wasn't prison. Questions continued to nag Pricilla. What had Claire hoped for in killing him? Revenge? Freedom?

He reached down and kissed her on the cheek. "I'm meeting Trisha downstairs in a few minutes, so I'd better get going."

Pricilla rested her hand on his arm. "Can I ask you a question first?"

"Of course." He leaned against the wall. "What is it?"

"Why do you think she did it? Claire, I mean. Why do you think she killed her husband?"

He shrugged a shoulder. "Does it really matter? I mean, she's admitted to the crime and the authorities have arrested her. She had motive and opportunity. As to exactly why. . .I suppose we'll never know."

She shook her head. She wanted answers. "I don't understand what would motivate a person to commit such a dreadful act. On the surface, Claire had everything. Money, success, beauty. . .but obviously none of that was enough. She wanted more and, for whatever reason, believed that with Charles out of the way, she'd find it."

Nathan scratched his chin. "Think about it. Are success and riches ever enough? Most people spend their whole lives searching for something they can never keep. They don't seem to realize that we enter into the world with nothing and we all leave this world with nothing."

" 'Store up for yourselves treasures in heaven.' " She quoted the verse from the book of Matthew and wrinkled her brow. "Is that the answer then? Claire was too caught up in getting ahead in life that she failed to look at the consequences?"

"And failed to realize that the stakes are bigger than making it financially, or climbing to the top of the social ladder." Nathan drew in a deep breath. "I think you need to let it go."

She nodded. "I know."

She glanced at the closed door. He was right, of course, but that didn't change the fact that it still beckoned her to open it. There would be no answers inside Claire's room as to why she'd done what she'd done, but the pull to investigate was there all the same.

She cleared her throat and decided to ask one last question. "There's one other thing that's been bothering me. A small detail of the case that was never resolved. If Simon Wheeler and Anthony Mills lost their business, how did they manage to pay for this expensive week?"

Nathan's brow rose at the question. "If I remember correctly, the entire week's bill was paid by the third party in their group, Michael Smythe."

Once again, questions began to surface as to the connection between Charles Woodruff and the three businessmen, but with Claire's confession, there obviously wasn't a link between the three men and Charles's death.

"Anything else?"

"No, just enjoy yourself."

"You don't have to worry about that. I'll see you later."

Pricilla watched Nathan slip down the stairs and out of view. The hallway was empty now, giving her the opportunity to do one final thing with the investigation before she could put it behind her. Pulling the master key from her pocket, she slipped it into the lock and turned the knob.

Inside, she went to the window and drew back the curtains, letting a flood of morning sunshine filter into the room. Misty hadn't come to clean yet, but the detective had emptied the room of all of Claire's possessions. It was a bleak reminder that Claire would not be coming back.

This time, there were no details of the room to consider. No pairs of shoes, or makeup, or jewelry. Columbo would find that one last scrap of evidence that would explain why Claire had made that fateful decision. The one thing that had been nagging at his mind that would pull all the pieces of the puzzle together and explain the case.

But there wasn't anything to find. Claire had confessed and, depending on a judge's pronouncement, she'd likely spend the next few decades behind bars. Taking one last look around the room, Pricilla sighed and opened the door. Max and Nathan, as usual, were right. It was time to give up her role of detective.

Penelope whisked passed her legs and into the room.

"Not now, Penelope." Pricilla spun around. "You're going to get me into trouble if I get caught snooping in here."

The cat slipped under the bed. Pricilla eyed the open door. Someone was coming up the steps. She shut the door then turned back to find the cat. Of all days for Penelope to pull one of her stunts. But she couldn't leave her here.

She bent down beside the bed, one leg at a time. Her hip protested, but she ignored the ache. "Penelope. Come here, kitty, kitty."

The cat lay contentedly beyond her grasp.

And that wasn't all that lay under that bed. She was going to have to remind Misty to do a better job at cleaning under the beds. Besides a number of dust bunnies, there was an ink pen, two earrings, and several pills.

Pricilla grabbed the pills and sat up, hitting her head on the edge of the nightstand.

"Ouch!"

The pain faded quickly as she stared at the two small pills. There had been a bottle of vitamins sitting on the nightstand the day she first tried questioning Claire. The event replayed clearly in her mind. The woman had knocked them over, spilling the contents across the thick carpet. Something had bothered Pricilla then, but she hadn't been able to put a finger on it. Holding the capsules in the palm of her hand, she pulled herself up onto the bed then adjusted her bifocals.

Pricilla might not be licensed to run the local pharmacy, but between her collection of herbal and prescription pills and those of her friends, she was quite certain of two things. One, these were the pills Claire had spilled, and two, these pills were not vitamins. She studied the markings closely. She'd bet her bottle of elderberry capsules that these were natural herbs used as a diuretic, the same ones, in fact, her good friend Marge took. Claire had implied that these were the pills that had killed Charles. And that she'd paid a fortune for the slow-acting poison. Pricilla was grasping at straws, and she knew it, but something wasn't adding up. The case was closed, and she might still be looking for a way to save Claire, but the question still remained. Penelope stole out from under the bed and rubbed against Pricilla's legs. Could Claire have inadvertently been giving her husband something quite harmless instead of the poison she thought she was giving him?

If that was true, then someone else had murdered Charles Woodruff.

16

Max took a bite of the muffin and kept his gaze on the *Rendezvous Sentinel*'s sports page in front of him. His mind, though, was elsewhere. He'd waited far too long to state his intentions to Pricilla and no matter what today brought, this was going to be the day he told her how he felt. No more excuses. No more looking for ways a relationship at their age couldn't work. And no more getting sidetracked by another one of her wild goose chases. Charles Woodruff's death had been solved, he had a lunch date with Pricilla, and while the Rendezvous Bar and Grill might not be the most romantic setting he could think of, once he told her how he felt he hoped it wouldn't matter.

"Max?"

He smiled. Pricilla stood in the doorway, wearing a tiger print, loose-fitting pants suit. Most women would have avoided the boldest outfit on the rack, but it looked perfect on her.

While he felt sorry for Claire Woodruff, he was admittedly glad she was in jail. Today, he'd have Pricilla all to himself, and he would have time to go forward with his own matchmaking plans. If they were as successful as the schemes they had hatched for Trisha and Nathan, there might even be something permanent in store for him and Pricilla in the near future.

"You're looking a tad more chipper." He patted the seat next to him. "Did you get some breakfast?"

"I can't think about food right now." Pricilla waved away the offer with her hand. "Claire might be innocent."

"Oh no." Max held the newspaper back up in front of his face, wishing he could momentarily disappear.

Claire had been sent to the slammer. . .locked in the poky. . .thrown in the penitentiary. . .case closed. So that meant Pricilla had *not* just said that Claire Woodruff was innocent, because it wasn't true. It couldn't be.

Pricilla slid into the chair next to him at the breakfast table and jabbed at the black-and-white newsprint. "Didn't you hear me?"

"I heard someone say that Claire was innocent, which can't be true," he said behind the cover of the paper. "So I'll have to say no."

Pricilla poked harder at the paper, her finger ripping a hole through tomorrow's weather forecast.

"Pricilla." He lowered the paper slowly then folded it into quarters, reminding himself that this was the woman he loved, and that her quirkiness just made her all the more endearing. Didn't it?

"I'm serious, Max. I think Claire might be innocent." She dropped two small pills on the white tablecloth and beamed in triumph.

He didn't get it. "Don't tell me this is your proof."

"Just hear me out."

He knew he didn't have a choice. So much for his grand plans of declaring his undying love to her without any distractions or interruptions. By the time he managed to tell her how he felt, he would be locked away in a retirement home.

He rested his elbows on the table. "Go ahead."

Pricilla leaned forward, her face looking as solemn as his commanding officers who sent him off to the Korean War. Not a good sign. She was dead serious.

"First of all," Pricilla began, "I admit that I might simply feel sorry for the woman and want to absolve Claire from her husband's death, but that doesn't change the fact that something doesn't add up."

"What doesn't add up?" He forced himself to look interested as he asked the question. He didn't want to go through this again. "The woman confessed to her husband's murder. Period. Case closed."

She held up a finger in her defense. "And how many people have confessed to crimes they either didn't commit or, as in Claire's case, thought they committed but really didn't?"

"You're kidding me, right? Why would she do that?" The room started slowly spinning in circles, as if the earth had finally fallen off its axis. "You're telling me that you think she only *believes* she committed the murder, but in reality she didn't?"

For the first time, Pricilla smiled. "So you do understand?"

His eyes narrowed. "Not at all."

She laid her hand on his arm, and he tried to ignore the effect she had on him. How could this woman make his heart race like he was nineteen again, while at the same time drive him insane with her off-the-wall ideas?

"Just listen to the facts, Max. Claire said she found a seller who sold her a slow-acting poison that cost a lot of money. What if this seller took advantage of Claire, and instead of giving her the poison, substituted it for a harmless drug so he'd make more money off of her?" She held up the pills in her hands. "Like these pills."

She still wasn't making any sense. "Where did you get these?"

"The day I went up to talk to Claire about the murder, she knocked over a bottle of vitamins. Something bothered me about the experience at the time, but I couldn't put my finger on it. Today, under her bed, I found two of the same pills from the bottle she knocked over—except that these aren't vitamins. That's what had been niggling at the back of my mind. If I'm not mistaken, these are the same pills that my friend Marge takes. Diuretics. A relatively harmless pill, for most people. Certainly not anything that would poison someone over a matter of weeks and then kill him."

He struggled to put the pieces together. "And how do you know that those are the pills she gave him, thinking they were poison?"

"I don't for sure, but she said she put the pills in a vitamin bottle because she knew he'd take them without complaining, and I only saw one vitamin bottle. And when she knocked it over, she acted jumpy, like she didn't want me to discover that there weren't really vitamins inside the bottle. Of course, she thought they were poison, even more reason for me not to see them."

Max rubbed his temples. He was worried because he was beginning to understand what she was saying. How was it that Pricilla could manage to make her theory sound so logical? Surely there was little merit to the idea, but what if she was right? Was the real murderer getting off scot-free? The thought sent a shiver down his spine. He had wanted to put this entire ordeal behind him, but Pricilla, as usual, had other ideas.

He didn't want to let himself agree with her logic. Not this time. "I still think you need to leave things alone. If we have to, we can go and talk to the detective. Tell him what you found and let him handle it."

She crossed her legs and leaned against the back of the chair. "I have a plan first."

A plan? Max tapped his fingers against the table. Of course she had a plan.

"My theory is easy enough to prove. I want to go into town and have the pills analyzed at the pharmacy. Then I want to talk to Claire in jail."

Thirty minutes later, Pricilla stood in line at the local pharmacy with the two pills in a plastic bag. Max stood beside her, his face grim. She couldn't blame him. He wasn't the only one frustrated that the case wasn't closed. Frustrated that there might be one missing piece that could completely change the outcome of the investigation. The only thing that made her smile was the fact that all her hard work as an undercover detective might actually pay off.

Not that she wanted to ever be involved in a murder investigation again. Not at all. She'd come to that conclusion at four o'clock this morning when she was lying in bed, wide awake. Frankly, her experiences in investigating Charles Woodruff's murder had left her believing that crime solving really should be left to the authorities—except perhaps Detective Carter—and that her ability to find this possible significant piece of the case was nothing more than a coincidence.

An elderly gentleman took his prescription from the pharmacist, leaving her free to speak to the middle-aged woman.

"I have a rather odd question, I'm afraid." Pricilla set the bag of pills down on the counter. "I need to know exactly what these are."

The woman chuckled and tucked a strand of her short hair behind her ear. "You'd be surprised how often people ask me that very question. Pills get dumped in their purse or onto the carpet—"

Pricilla cleared her throat. "Well, I'm certainly glad I'm not the only one who's ever asked."

"These are diuretics." The pharmacist held up the

pills in her hand. "They're used for removing water from the body by—"

"Thank you. I do know what a diuretic is, I was just afraid it might be something a bit more—" Max thumped her foot with the end of his crutch, and she switched the direction of the conversation. "Anyway, thank you. I know how important it is to keep one's prescription medicines straight."

"It's very important. Please don't hesitate to ask if you have questions like this again."

Max followed her out to the car. "You've got to learn when it's time to ask a question and when it's time to be quiet."

She ignored his reprimand. "We got our answer, didn't we? These pills couldn't have killed Charles Woodruff, and if Claire confirms that this was what she gave her husband, then there's another murderer on the loose."

After a quick stop at the instant photo booth tourists used on Main Street, Pricilla pulled into the driveway of the sheriff's office. Max hobbled behind her toward the glass doors that led to the small detention facility on the west side of the building.

"I don't get it, Pricilla." She could hear him huffing as he struggled up the sidewalk. "Secret photos and one of your cakes?"

She caught his odd expression, surprised he'd held off his questions this long. "Both are a part of my plan."

Max stopped along the cement walk. "They're not going to let you give food to an inmate, and—"

"Don't worry." Pricilla kept on walking. "The cake's not for Claire."

"I don't think they allow you to bribe the officials either," Max mumbled, but she was already through the glass doors.

He let out a sharp breath then hurried to catch up with her. If she wasn't careful, he'd end up visiting her behind bars. He could see the headlines now: WOMAN ARRESTED FOR ATTEMPTING TO BRIBE LOCAL AUTHORITIES WITH SLICE OF SUCCULENT CAKE. . . .

By the time he got inside, she was standing in front of a row of lockers.

"Can you believe this?"

"What?"

"We can't take anything inside if we want to see one of the inmates." She jiggled the key on the locker. "Do you have a quarter? I used the last of mine at the photo booth."

"A quarter." Max fished some change out of his pocket then handed her the coin.

He should have stayed home. At least then he could be lounging on the front porch of the lodge with a good book and a plate of Pricilla's cookies, instead of chasing empty clues.

She dumped her coat and her purse into the metal box then headed toward the reception desk with the cake.

He decided not to even ask.

"Detective Carter." Patricia greeted the man matter-of-factly.

"Ah, Mrs. Crumb. I wasn't expecting to see you today."

"We're here to visit Claire Woodruff," Pricilla announced to the balding detective.

The officer scratched the back of his head. "First of all, the only thing that you're allowed to bring in here are your keys and identification. There are lockers on the other side of the glass doors where you can store your things."

"I understand, but first let me ask you if it's possible to see Claire."

The man shoved his glasses up the bridge of his nose. "You have to have an appointment before you're allowed to visit with one of our inmates."

"I don't have an appointment. Would you—"

"Appointments need to be made twenty-four hours in advance."

"Wait a minute." Pricilla shook her head. "Mrs. Woodruff was only arrested last night, so there was no way that I could have made an appointment twenty-four hours ago."

"Well, then, only family can see her, and I know for certain that you are *not* family." The detective picked up his pen. "I can make an appointment for you for next Wednesday."

"Next Wednesday?"

"And don't bring anything into this lobby with you next time, or you won't be allowed to visit."

"It's just a cake." She held it out to him, as if the scent of the citrus would change his mind. "One of my lemon crumb cakes."

"That's nice, but it's still not allowed. No snacks, packages, drugs, or contraband for our inmates."

Her lips curved into a frown. "I wouldn't consider my cake contraband, and besides, it's not for one of your inmates."

"Pricilla, I think we should leave now," Max prompted, but she stood her ground.

"Is the sheriff back in town?" she asked.

Max cocked his head. *What was this? Plan B?*

The detective glanced toward one of the back offices. "He's on duty right now."

"I'd like to see him, please."

Max wondered if he should turn around and walk right out the door and wait for her in the car. Doing things the proper way would be too simple when Pricilla was involved. But, he had to admit, not nearly as interesting.

A minute later, a stocky officer with graying hair strode across the lobby. "Mrs. Crumb! It's such a pleasure to see you."

Max couldn't help but smile to himself. Of course.

Pricilla had an inside contact. Why had he ever questioned the fact that she had a plan?

"Sheriff Tucker. How was your trip back East?" Pricilla grasped the man's hands.

"Great, but it's always good to be home. I arrived back in town last night."

"And your wife and that precious granddaughter of yours? How are they?"

The sheriff pulled his wallet out of his back pocket and flipped it open to a picture of a sleeping infant. "They're both fine, thank you. It's hard to believe, but little Hailey will be four weeks old next Sunday."

Pricilla glanced at the department store photo and grinned. "She's grown so much and is positively adorable. Sheriff, I want you to meet my dear friend, Max Summers. He's up visiting from New Mexico."

"It's nice to meet you, Mr. Summers."

Max reached out to shake his hand. "Nice to meet you, too."

"I know Sheriff Tucker from church," Pricilla said. "Some of the ladies organized a few meals to help out when his daughter was in the hospital, delivering Hailey."

"A couple meals?" The sheriff shoved his wallet back into his pocket and laughed. "This woman could feed an army with the food she brought my kids. Allowed me to sample a few of the dishes. Juicy ribs, roast with gravy and mashed potatoes. . ."

The descriptions were enough to make Max's stomach growl. "No one would argue that Pricilla is an excellent cook."

A blush crept up Pricilla's face as she picked up the cake off the counter. "The detective here implied that I shouldn't have brought a cake, but after promising you I'd make you and your wife one, I hadn't thought that there would be a problem for me to bring it to you at the station."

"Of course it's not a problem." The sheriff took the dessert and smiled. "Can I sneak a piece before I clock out tonight?"

"I'll leave that for you and your conscience to settle. I know how much your wife loves lemon cake." Pricilla laughed. "Now Sheriff, there is one other thing—"

Max leaned against the counter, eager to see what would happen next. Pricilla was obviously born with an extra measure of charm, because considering the pleased expression on the sheriff's face, he looked as if he would grant her anything she asked for. Detective Carter, on the other hand, wasn't looking quite as compliant.

"We're here to see Claire Woodruff," Pricilla began. "She had been a guest at my son's lodge and doesn't know a soul in the area. We'd really like to see her if it wouldn't be too much trouble."

"Well, there are rules, you know, that even one of your lemon crumb cakes can't get around." The sheriff laughed again, and his belly shook. "You'll have to wait until visiting hours start, but I don't see a problem in waiving the twenty-four hour rule in this case. Do you, Carter?"

"I. . .of course not."

Pricilla clasped her hands together. "I certainly appreciate it, Sheriff. I've just been so worried about the woman. "

"We will have to see a photo ID and run a background check. Regulations, you know, even for people we're acquainted with. But my nephew here will take care of that, and then you can see her in about forty-five minutes if she's in agreement."

Pricilla noted Carter's grimace, but forty-five minutes later, he ushered her and Max into a pale green room lined with chairs. The detective told them where to sit, and it was another five minutes before he led Claire into the room.

The detective stood at the door. "Visitation will be over in exactly thirty minutes."

Claire walked toward them slowly, looking surprised. Her face was pale and there were bags under her eyes. "How nice of you to come by. I—"

"Are you all right?" Pricilla frowned, wishing she could have bit back the words the moment they'd surfaced. Of course the woman wasn't all right. She'd been arrested for killing her husband and now faced a lifetime behind bars. "I'm sorry. I shouldn't have asked such an insensitive question."

Claire sat down on the edge of the seat and rubbed her hands against the legs of her orange prison garb. "I've just gone from socialite to jail inmate. You can't go much lower than that."

Max leaned forward. "What about your bond?"

"My case is supposed to go before a judge today and my lawyer's getting my money together. Some of Charles's assets have been frozen, but thankfully it shouldn't be a problem. I'd sell my right arm to get out of here if I had to."

Pricilla squeezed her hand. "Maybe it won't be that difficult."

Claire's brow narrowed. "What do you mean?"

Max nudged Pricilla with his elbow and she nodded slightly. He was right. She was going to have to be careful about what she said. For all she knew, this was going to turn into nothing more than another dead end.

Pricilla pulled from her pocket the photo she'd taken of the two pills, and showed it to Claire. The clarity wasn't perfect, but it was good enough for what she needed. "I found these pills under your bed at the lodge. I need to know if these are the same pills you used to poison your husband."

Claire covered her hand with her mouth and nodded her head. "I don't want to think about it."

"Claire, I know you're upset, but I need you to listen to me very carefully. I don't know where you got these pills, but they are simply a mild diuretic."

"No." She wrung her hands together. "The man I bought them from told me they were a slow-acting poison. He couldn't guarantee how long it would take for them to work, but he assured me they would."

Pricilla looked to Max. There was one more thing she had to ask.

"I have one more question for you. Is it possible that whoever sold you the pills was simply trying to extract money from you?" She patted her pocket. "These pills couldn't have poisoned Charles."

Pricilla studied the woman's face. Instead of relief, though, she saw fear in Claire's eyes. A lab test would prove for certain what the pills were, but her previous theory now moved to the forefront. If Claire didn't kill her husband, then who did?

17

Max slid into the booth across from Pricilla and tapped his fingers against the brown Formica table. Just when the murder of Charles Woodruff had come to a nice and neat conclusion, Pricilla had managed to find a way to blow the case wide open with two tiny diuretic pills.

He picked up the plastic menu and studied the lunch items. Ham, roast beef, meatloaf. . . His stomach growled. There might be a murderer on the loose, but he still had his appetite. The Rendezvous Bar and Grill had been overly crowded, so he'd suggested they stop for lunch at Tiffany's. The small café, located just off Main Street, was quiet, and he hoped for a chance to talk to Pricilla about something besides Charles Woodruff's death—namely, the fact that he had waited far too long to declare his intentions toward her.

But there was another issue that had to be resolved before he could bring any plans of romance into the conversation.

He looked up at her and caught her gaze. "You know we have to talk to the detective about what you found out from Claire."

She pulled off her coat and laid it on the seat beside her. "Yes, but I thought we should discuss the new development first."

He had no desire to discuss the details of the case. While he could see that Pricilla actually might be on to something with her diuretic pills, that didn't change the fact that this was the detective's investigation. Not theirs. And Max was finished playing her bumbling sidekick.

She pulled out her compact and dabbed powder on her nose. "I want to be able to give the detective something more. If nothing else, a well thought out theory so he won't simply dismiss what I have to say as the ramblings of some crazy old woman looking to be the next Jessica Fletcher."

"No one thinks you're a crazy old woman."

She grinned, and his heart thudded offbeat in a peculiar rhythm that might have had him worried under other circumstances. He didn't know why, exactly, but there was no doubt that Pricilla had stolen his heart. With all her quirks and eccentricities, she'd managed to not only step in and fill the lonely ache inside him, but give him a reason to smile again. He'd never believed that growing older meant growing old, and she was the perfect antidote to life this side of middle age.

Pricilla hugged the menu to her chest. "If Claire really is innocent, I need to come up with a solid hypothesis on who committed the crime. While I never liked Oscar, he doesn't seem to have a strong motive for murder. What do you think?"

He glanced again at the daily special and decided on meatloaf and mashed potatoes before answering her question. "There were definite underlying hostilities between the two men, but no matter who actually killed Charles, you can't forget that Claire's far from innocent."

She frowned. "I suppose you are right, though I admit that I'd hoped that in the end Claire would be absolved of all wrongdoing."

"Intent can be just as deadly as the actual crime."

Pricilla sighed and signaled for the waitress. "Are you thirsty, Max? I think I need a strong cup of coffee before I can even think about eating lunch."

He nodded and two minutes later, he was sipping black coffee and mentally strategizing his next move. A move that had nothing to do with Pricilla's continuing investigation. He'd rehearsed the conversation a thousand times in his mind.

Pricilla—he'd look deep into her eyes as he spoke— *we've known each other a long time, and despite the fact that we always lived miles apart, our families still managed to go through many of life's ups and downs together. From raising teenagers, to empty nests, to the loss of our spouses, to retirement. . . I don't know how you will feel about this, but I'd like to see our relationship move beyond friendship. I'm sixty-five years old, but you make me feel as if I'm thirty-five again. And while I never thought that I would feel this way again, if you're willing to take a chance—*

"On the other hand, the real murderer could be Simon or Anthony." Pricilla leaned forward and rested her elbows on the table, jerking him from his thoughts as she spoke. "They had a strong motive as well as opportunity."

"They were always near the top of my suspect list." Max stopped then frowned. She had done it again. Pulled him off track from his task at hand. How could one woo a lady's heart when she had murder on her mind? "Pricilla."

"I do have a theory—"

"Pricilla." He took a deep breath. "I don't want to talk about Claire right now. I don't want to talk about Charles Woodruff, or anyone who might have killed him. Not Oscar, or Anthony, or Simon—"

"All right." She knitted her brow together and shot him a confused expression. "What do you want to talk about?"

"Us." Max cringed the moment he spoke. He'd planned to be subtle at first, but instead he'd blurted it out.

"Us?"

He cleared his throat and fiddled with his half-empty mug. "I didn't mean it to come out so. . .so stern, but yes. Us. The truth is, I care about you as a woman, and a friend, but I've come to realize that I care about you in a far deeper way, as well. I know we're past the age most people think about falling in love, but that's just it. I love being with you. And I've fallen in love with you. In spite of the craziness of this week, I've been happy because I'm with you."

Her eyes widened, but he'd gotten this far and there was no turning back now. "I'm sure this comes as a bit of a surprise, and I'm not asking for you to say anything you're not ready to, but if you've ever considered the idea of something developing between us, even for a moment, then. . .well, just think about it."

~~~~~

Pricilla was certain her heart was going to explode. Had he just declared his intentions toward her? For a moment she didn't think she was going to be able to take another breath.

Max Summers loved her.

He loved her?

She gulped in a deep breath of air and took in the woodsy scent of his cologne. Shaking her head, she tried to pull her thoughts together. She'd never thought about Max romantically. Or had she? It was true that she'd been affected by the same bright blue eyes that stared at her right now. And if she was honest with herself, her pulse had fluttered a time or two, and her heart had pounded at least once at his dimpled grin. Then there had been the embarrassing scene with Misty when she'd believed that the young woman had her sights set on Max—

Pricilla had convinced herself that there weren't feelings of interest on her part, but because they were in the middle of a murder investigation, everything had been knocked off kilter. Could her reactions be proof that she felt something deeper as well?

Max's face turned a pale shade of gray. "I didn't mean to be so abrupt, but I've waited long enough to tell you how I feel."

And she'd waited too long to respond. "You just. . . you just caught me off guard."

"Have you ever thought about something developing between us beyond the friendship we share?"

"I don't know. I—"

The waitress chose that moment to come take their order. Pricilla would have preferred for her and Max to leave so they could find a place to talk without any interruptions. His declaration had her mind spinning in opposite directions, but instead she settled on a toasted cheese sandwich and a side salad, hoping she'd still be able to eat when the food arrived.

Once the waitress had left, he grasped her hands and caught her gaze.

"I don't want to lose our friendship, Pricilla, but I'm not getting any younger. I want to take a chance to find happiness again. . .with you."

Her heart fluttered. If she were honest with herself, there was no one she enjoyed being around more. Max made her feel cherished and appreciated. Who said you have to be twenty to fall in love?

Love?

The word surprised her, but for the first time Pricilla realized that the comfortable relationship she had developed with Max throughout the years had turned into that very thing.

She was in love with Max. And he was in love with her.

The thought brought a smile to her lips. What that meant to their future, she had no idea, but for the moment, it didn't matter. "Do you remember when you caught me eavesdropping on you and Misty?"

He laughed. "It was a scene I'll likely never forget."

"I was jealous of Misty."

"What?"

Confessions of guilt weren't normally her forte, but for some reason it was important for him to know. "Misty is pretty, outgoing, half my age. . .and she was coming on to you."

"No, she wasn't."

Pricilla cocked her head and raised the pitch of her voice. "I'm looking for someone much more stable. Someone older who realizes—"

"All right." He shook his head and grinned. "Enough—"

"Someone like you, Max."

"I said enough." There was a twinkle in his eye. "So, I haven't taken you totally by surprise?"

"No, I am totally surprised, yet looking back, I think I've felt the same way for quite some time and never knew it."

He squeezed her hands, and she wondered what was in store for the two of them. Life had become comfortable, even predictable—barring the recent murder, of course— and the thought of something new on the horizon sent a shiver of excitement down her spine.

The waitress placed their orders in front of them. Pricilla stared at her plate. There was one thing she still had to ask him.

"What happens now?" She picked up her fork and pushed a piece of tomato around. "You're leaving in a couple of days, and I don't think either of us is ready to make a huge move at this point."

Max shrugged. "All I know is that the very questions you're probably asking yourself right now are the same questions that have kept me from telling you how I feel. And trust me, I've thought of all the reasons why a relationship between us won't work. We're too old, too set in our ways, live too many miles apart. . . Yet I'm convinced we can figure out a way to make this work."

"I know you're right."

He said a prayer for the food then dug into his meatloaf. "So, what is your theory?"

There was a look of contentment on his face, but she was still reeling over his statement and was having a hard time getting her mind focused back on lunch, let alone the Woodruff case. "My theory?"

"You said you had a theory."

Trying to settle her mind, she put the cloth napkin in her lap. What was her theory?

She chuckled. "It's not fair to take me completely off guard with thoughts of love and romance then ask me my theories on the murder investigation."

"Then how about we spend the rest of lunch without any mention of Claire, or the case?"

"Agreed."

Max reached out and squeezed Pricilla's hand. No matter what happened with the rest of the investigation, she knew one thing was certain. Life would never be the same again.

18

For the second time that day, Pricilla pulled the car into the gravel parking lot in front of the sheriff's office. A storm gathered in the distance, but for now, warm rays of sunshine still filtered through the darkening clouds above them, helping to lessen the sharp chill of the afternoon breeze. She turned off the car and glanced at Max.

He still carried himself as a commanding officer. Pressed shirt and slacks, military haircut, broad shoulders and upright posture that gave him an air of authority. . . Falling in love again had not been on her agenda. It was hard to imagine that so much had changed between them in such a short time.

She raised her head toward the glass doors of the building. Her interest in the Woodruff case had waned somewhat since Max's confession. Not that she wasn't still intent on finding out the truth, but her feelings toward Max had taken a sudden precedence, and she was having a hard time formulating exactly what she wanted to tell the sheriff. Formulating *any* of her thoughts for that matter.

Max opened his door and reached for the crutches. "Are you coming?"

"I think so." She pushed back an errant curl from the side of her face. "I'm still a little dazed from our conversation at lunch."

Part of her told her his confession of love had been nothing more than a figment of her imagination—but his nervous smile told her otherwise.

"I suppose it is a bit awkward." He pulled his door shut, stopping the sound of the howling wind. "That was one thing that made me hesitate to say anything to you sooner." His eyes darkened. "I've been worried that in telling you how I feel, I'd ruin our friendship—"

"No. It's not that at all." She tapped her hands against the steering wheel. Knowing what to say had rarely been a problem, but sitting beside him, discussing their relationship, left her feeling like a tongue-tied teenager. "You've awakened feelings I didn't know I had, and now I'm trying to untangle them all. Does that make any sense?"

Max chuckled. "Complete sense. But all we have to do is take things a day at a time and see what happens."

She nodded and opened her door, realizing that it was time now to see what would happen when she told the detective about the two little pills that might change the entire direction of the case. Something she was dreading to have to do, because she had a feeling that the detective wasn't going to be keen on her findings now that he thought the case had been wrapped up nicely like an early birthday present.

As Pricilla hurried into the building, letting Max hold the door for her, she felt the heat rise in her cheeks over his chivalrous action. Which was ridiculous. Max was a gentleman and always held the door for ladies. It was the realization that he was doing it for her as a part of a courting ritual that had her feeling tingly from head to toe.

Inside the sterile reception, she was disappointed to see Detective Carter standing behind the reception desk with no sign of the sheriff. On her way up the sidewalk, she'd decided that if at all possible she'd bypass the detective with her information, even though he'd been technically in charge of the case.

"Good afternoon again, Detective." She set her purse down. "Is the sheriff still in?"

"Nope. He'll be out the rest of the day." The detective picked up a folder then leaned against the desk with a sigh. "Is there something else you need, Mrs. Crumb? Visiting hours are over until Saturday."

"I'm not here to see Claire, but I suppose if the sheriff is gone, then I will need to speak to you." She swallowed her disappointment. "It's regarding the Woodruff case."

"Of course." His stern expression made it perfectly clear that he wasn't pleased with the interruption. "Mrs. Crumb, if you've forgotten, the initial investigation will more than likely be officially closed by the end of the day. Then Mrs. Woodruff will be arraigned and her preliminary hearing date set."

Pricilla gnawed on the edge of her lip. "I don't know how to say this, other to come straight out and tell you. I don't believe Mrs. Woodruff killed her husband."

"Mrs. Crumb"—the detective folded his arms across his chest and shook his head—"I realize that you have been playing the part of an investigator during this case, and that's fine for fiction and the movies, but this is real life. And in real life, it's the law that handles cases like Mrs. Woodruff's. Not a novice detective like yourself."

Pricilla felt her blood pressure rise as she fought to control her growing temper. "Detective Carter, I resent your implications that I—"

Max leaned over and nudged her gently. His reminders were becoming far too frequent, though even she admitted to the fact that she needed someone to keep her in line when it came to the balding detective.

She decided to start again. "Will you just let me explain?"

He glanced at his watch. "You have exactly one minute."

Pricilla frowned, but her determination didn't waiver. She set the bag of pills on the counter, and told him step-by-step what she'd discovered both at the lodge and from Claire this morning.

"So, if these were the pills Claire was using to poison her husband, and they're nothing more than water pills, the conclusion is quite obvious. Claire Woodruff might have intended to dispose of Charles, but what she gave him was harmless."

The detective stared at her, his arms still crossed until she finished. "And that's it?"

"That's what?"

"Did you consider that fact that Mrs. Woodruff is used to living life among the upper class? She probably has a large home, expensive cars, and all the similar trappings of money. But murder is a serious crime, and she's intelligent enough to try and find a way out." He leaned forward, resting his hands against the desk. "Confession might relieve the soul, but when the reality of what she's done begins to sink in, I'm not surprised at all at her attempts to get you on her side with this. . .this concocted plan to set a guilty woman free."

"Excuse me?" Pricilla's eyes widened. "She didn't come to me with a concocted plan to get out of jail. The woman was genuinely surprised when I told her what I'd discovered."

The detective took a step back, obviously debating whether or not he should consider her story.

She, on the other hand, wasn't finished stating her case. "If I'm correct, then by your doing nothing, the real murderer could very well be running free tonight. I also know your uncle well enough to recognize that he will be quite impressed when he finds out that he followed through on a lead and ended up cracking the case and finding the real offender."

He shook his head. "What if you're wrong?"

She held his gaze. "What if I'm right?"

She'd hit a nerve with the detective, she could tell. He took the pills and dropped them into an envelope. "We have the rest of the contents from their room at the lodge, so it will only be a matter of time before we find any discrepancies, if there are indeed any to be found."

"Perhaps. But then again, perhaps not."

Max cleared his throat. "I think it's time we headed back to the lodge."

"I was just thinking the same thing." Pricilla nodded her head. "Good day, Detective Carter."

Pricilla waited until they were outside and out of earshot from the detective before she spoke again. "I can't imagine where that man got his manners. Certainly not from his uncle. At least we still have our list of possible suspects. Now it's up to us to set a trap for the murderer."

Max slid into the front seat of the car, trying to decipher Pricilla's last comment. He'd hoped that by going to the sheriff's office and informing the detective of what they'd found out, she'd give up any ideas of pursuing a possible second murderer. He'd also hoped, if nothing else, that his confession over lunch would be a strong enough distraction to convince her to leave things alone. Now, he wasn't sure it was.

He glanced at her out of the corner of his eye as she drove down the main street of town. Past the *Rendezvous Sentinel*'s offices. Past the Starlight Theater, Allie's Antiques, and the Baker's Dozen, a bakery that threw in an extra item for every dozen you bought.

Tourists loved the quaint, old-fashioned look of the town that boasted numerous bed and breakfasts and three nearby ski resorts. Up until now, the town of Rendezvous had also boasted of the fact that violent crime was virtually nonexistent. The thought that there was a murderer on the loose, who was staying at the lodge, no less, did little to ease his worry. All the more reason that the sheriff's office should handle things and not Pricilla, his self-appointed private investigator and novice detective.

She pulled onto the dirt road that headed out of town and toward the lodge. "You're awfully quiet."

"I've been thinking."

"So have I."

He frowned. "You're not seriously considering setting a trap to catch a murderer, Pricilla. Are you?"

"I still have a few details to work out, and I'm going to have to convince Nathan to call in a favor for me, but yes. I have a plan."

He forced himself to ask the question. "What is your plan?"

A smile tugged at the corners of her mouth. "Think about all the great literary detectives and how they pinned down the suspect. They all had a plan. A moment of truth when they forced a confession out of the suspect then pulled on the noose until the suspect had nowhere to run."

"And how do you expect to do this?"

"I had already planned dinner tonight to be a celebration. Everyone will be gathered together in the dining room, and just at the point when their appetites are satisfied, I'll stand and address the group."

Max winced as the bumpy road jostled the car and, in turn, his injured foot. Unfortunately, his foot wasn't his biggest concern at the moment. "So, you're planning the clichéd dinner party where the detective corners the murderer with his wit and intellectual brilliance."

"I wouldn't say it's a cliché."

"And I wouldn't say you're Sherlock Holmes."

His comment put a sour look on her face, but he didn't care. He wanted their relationship to have a happy ending—and it wasn't going to if she started accusing people of murder.

Pricilla pulled into the driveway of the lodge, knowing Max wasn't impressed with her idea. Maybe she was pushing things too far. She'd been lucky. . .or rather blessed. . .that nothing had happened to her during her informal interrogation of the suspects. But what could happen over beef burgundy and roasted vegetables, in a room full of people?

She parked the car and turned off the engine. "Are you mad at me?"

"For some reason, I've always had a hard time staying mad at you." As he gave her a lopsided grin, she felt a surge of relief shoot through her. "But that doesn't mean I'm ready for you to play the role of Sherlock Holmes."

"And why not, Dr. Watson? I've always thought we made a good team. And I promise not to do anything foolish."

His brows rose in question. "Is that something you can promise?"

"You have to admit that I've had at least one or two good ideas regarding the case so far."

He drew in a deep breath and let it out slowly. "You get Nathan's permission, and I'll back you up."

She smiled and got out of the car. There was something else to make her smile, as well. Nathan and Trisha sat on the porch together, enjoying the afternoon. She might not be certain what would happen between her and Max as far as their future, but she wouldn't be disappointed at all if wedding bells sounded in the future for their children, something that ranked far higher than solving the Woodruff case.

She sat down in a cushioned chair beside Max on the porch and addressed their children. "Hope you're enjoying the last of this weather. Looks like a storm will hit later this evening."

Trisha shivered and pulled her sweater around her shoulders. "The temperature has already begun to drop in the past thirty minutes, but I love watching the storms come in."

Nathan crossed his ankles and leaned back. "Where have the two of you been?"

Ignoring the twinkle in her son's eye, Pricilla glanced at Max. She'd tell Nathan later about what had happened in her own love life, but for now, they needed to deal with a much more serious matter.

"We've been at the sheriff's office," Pricilla began. "There have been some new developments in the case since last night, and there's a good chance that Claire didn't murder her husband."

"What?" Surprise marked Trisha's expression.

Briefly, Pricilla summarized the latest findings in the case.

When she was finished, Nathan shook his head. "You've got to be kidding. What does the detective say about all of this?"

Pricilla laughed. "He's skeptical, but I think he sees the merit in what I showed him."

Nathan slapped his hands against his thighs. "Just when I think the trouble's behind us, another threat pops up."

Pricilla smiled. She had hoped that the possible threat to the lodge would be motivation enough to get her son to agree to her idea. That last thing any of them wanted was for the lodge's reputation to be tarnished further. Solving the crime was the only way to guarantee that things would actually get back to normal.

"There's something else." She worked to keep her expression composed. "I need your help."

Nathan held up his hand. "Mom, I thought I told you to stay out of it. Let the detective do his job."

"All I'm planning is a simple dinner party. Everyone

else will think it's a celebration of the Woodruff case being closed. If we can catch the real murderer off guard, we might be able to find out the truth."

"Sounds a bit old-fashioned, if you ask me. I mean, with DNA analysis and forensic science, I'm not sure I see the value in simply trying to catch the murderer off guard." Her son turned to Max. "Don't tell me you're going along with this?"

"I don't think you're going to talk her out of it."

Worried lines crossed Nathan's brow. "So you agree that bringing a group of suspects together, like the last chapter of a mystery novel, including a possible murderer, is a good idea? That with a few, well-planned-out words we can actually catch the person who killed Charles Woodruff?"

Pricilla fidgeted in her chair. Nathan was weakening. She could see it in his eyes.

"You know your mother." Max glanced in her direction and winked. "She tends to be quite persuasive."

"Yes, I do." Pricilla puckered her brow. They were doing it again. Talking as if she weren't there.

"And knowing you, Mother, the idea will probably work."

She leaned forward. "So you'll help?"

"I don't suppose we have anything to lose? Tell me what you need me to do."

19

Pricilla set the last silver spoon on the table then stood back to admire the effect. Tonight, she'd decided against the normal stoneware place settings and their rustic forest scenes and decided instead to use the formal white dishes with the gold rim. She ran her hand across the smooth mauve tablecloth and smiled. With the table set and a buffet ready, the truth of who really killed Charles Woodruff was about to be discovered.

Rain tapped against the windows as the temperature outdoors continued to drop. Shivering, she added two logs to the fire and watched as the yellow flames came back to life. The atmosphere was perfect. She dimmed the overhead lights, and the crystal glasses caught the golden reflection of the fireplace. A flash of lightning lit up the floor-to-ceiling windows. Seconds later, thunder rumbled in the distance.

She checked her watch. It was fifteen minutes before seven. She had included Oscar and Misty on the guest list, and while the invitation might seem a bit unorthodox with the case closed and a mood of celebration in the air, she was convinced that no one would mind. The ease of the buffet would make the dinner elegant, yet simple enough to ensure that everyone had a good time.

Lighting the three ivory candles that made up the centerpiece, she then blew out the match, inhaling the woodsy scent of the smoke. Everything was ready.

Max entered the room early, giving her the extra boost of confidence she needed for the rest of the evening. He looked stunning in a gray suit jacket and paisley tie, the perfect attire for a formal dinner party. Perfect enough for her heart to thud and her knees to quiver at the site of him and his gorgeous blue eyes.

But as they both knew, she had something far different than a social—or romantic—occasion in mind tonight. A rush of adrenalin surged through her. She felt like Jessica Fletcher on the brink of solving one of her cases. And if her theory was right, Pricilla would prove to Detective Carter that while she might be a novice, her intuition was rarely off track.

Granted, she didn't have the authority of a badge to back her up, but she'd followed the clues of the case and interviewed the suspects until she'd discovered a loose end in the detective's theory. Who said that this gray-haired retiree needed to stick to card games and knitting needles to fill her time? She was about to prove them all wrong.

Max popped a crouton from the sideboard into his mouth. "Are you ready for this?"

"I think so." She nodded and drew in a slow, calming breath. "Do you think I'm doing the right thing?"

He leaned into his crutches. "You're staking a lot on your convictions, but that's one of the things

I admire about you the most. Your determination to stand up for justice, no matter what the cost."

Pricilla laughed. "You're making me seem far more noble than I feel. But you're right about one thing. While Claire might be guilty of intending to murder her husband, I honestly don't believe that she was the one who killed Charles. I just don't know if I can prove it."

"We will see, but hopefully, in the next hour or so, you'll be able to do just that."

Pricilla checked her watch and another wave of adrenalin shot through her. She tried to relax, but found it impossible. Ten more minutes. Then she'd either be able to prove her theory that Claire was innocent—or end up making a complete fool out of herself.

"Pricilla?"

She glanced up and realized she had missed something Max had said. "I'm sorry. I'm nervous."

"You don't have to go through with this—"

"No, I feel like I have to."

She rechecked the dishes on the sideboard to make sure she hadn't forgotten something from tonight's menu. It was simply the way she was. She couldn't stand for anything to be left undone. Solving Charles Woodruff's death was no different. Not finding out the truth at this point would be failure.

Convinced that everything was in order, she turned to Max. "Do you have any last minute theories?"

"Actually, I do." Max hobbled over to the fireplace and laid his crutches down before sitting on the stone hearth. "I spent a good hour online before coming down here, looking deeper into Simon and Anthony's failed business that Charles took over."

He had her full attention now. "And?"

"While I'm sure the detective has looked into the connection, I did find something very interesting. Simon's family owns a large orchard in western Colorado. They grow peaches, cherries, and have even started growing grapes in the past five years."

She lowered her brow, not yet following his theory. "So what's the connection?"

"Peach pits contain cyanide, and the leaves of certain cherry trees can also be highly poisonous—"

"And Detective Carter is certain that the final lab test will prove that Charles died of cyanide poisoning." Everything started to click together. Maybe she hadn't been that far off after all.

Max shrugged a shoulder. "Of course, I've also thought of the possibility that it's nothing more than a coincidence. From what I read online, it would take a lot of peach pits to kill a person."

"But if someone knew what they were doing—"

"True, but even the diuretic pills could be nothing more than a red herring. I still think that the most logical conclusion is that Claire is the guilty party."

Pricilla crossed the Oriental rug and stood in front of him. "Then let's pray that truth prevails tonight. I'm ready to put this behind me."

"I'm ready as well." He reached out and took

her hands. "Mainly, because there are a lot of other things I'd rather be discussing with you than Charles Woodruff."

Pricilla felt a blush cross her cheeks. "For instance?"

"Like what the future holds for you and me."

Her pulse quickened. He was right. There were still a lot of things they needed to talk about. While preparing dinner, she had mulled over the obstacles standing between them and still hadn't come to any firm conclusions as to what might work. The barriers that had made him hesitate to talk to her about his feelings in the first place hadn't disappeared because she'd admitted she shared his feelings. There were genuine concerns that would have to be dealt with, because a long-distance relationship was never the best solution.

But she wasn't sure how to change that. He'd mentioned things like being old and stubborn as well as the distance between them. Max hated the cold Colorado winters, and she didn't fancy the New Mexico summers. Then there was the lodge and the job she hoped would become permanent. Nathan needed her, and she needed something to keep her busy. Whatever she and Max decided in the end, it would take a whole lot of compromise from both of them.

He rubbed the back of her hand with his thumb. "You're not having second thoughts are you? About us, I mean."

"No." She smiled, certain that any compromises on her part would be worth it. "But you are right about the fact that there are a few complications we will have to look at."

"In the meantime, I think we both need to subscribe to a cheap phone plan."

"And take out stock in the U.S. Post Office." Pricilla laughed. "Have you thought about extending your trip?"

His smile dissolved into a frown. "If I hadn't promised to coordinate one of our local children's Christmas-toy drives this year, I'd consider it, but don't worry. I'm planning to return here soon."

"I'm counting on it."

Pricilla pulled her hands away from Max as Nathan entered the room with Trisha. It was time to push any ideas of romance aside and remember that there was a far more serious matter to deal with at the moment.

One by one the guests entered the dining room. The murmur of conversation and sporadic laughter filtered throughout the room as they began to fill their plates. Pricilla smiled in anticipation. They had no idea that she had set a trap for Charles Woodruff's real murderer, and if everything went according to plan, there would be a second arrest made tonight—and the Woodruff case would *finally* be closed.

She served herself from the buffet then sat beside Max at the table. Eating slowly, she enjoyed the beef, the roasted vegetables, and rice pilaf—but her mind was elsewhere as she studied the guests. Anthony roared with amusement as he threw out the punch line of some hunting joke. His buddies, Simon and Michael, joined in the laughter. None of them looked as if they'd recently been involved in a deed as grim as murder. Instead, they were probably thinking about how relieved they were to be leaving in the morning for their long-awaited hunting trip.

Oscar, looking as if he felt out of place, chuckled at something Anthony said the far end of the table. Undoubtedly, he would prefer to be out tracking game rather than dressing in a button-down shirt and slacks to attend a formal dinner. Nathan and Trisha were deep in their own conversation and looked as if they'd forgotten that the rest of them were in the room. Even Misty seemed to be enjoying herself as she filled her plate with another helping of food.

At seven forty-five, the guests began to push back their plates, contented expressions on their faces. Satisfied that the timing was perfect, Pricilla tapped her glass and moved to stand behind her chair. Clearing her throat, she attempted to address the group formally, as Hercule Poirot might have done when wrapping up one of his own famous cases.

"Before dessert is served, I'd like to make an announcement." She gripped the curved back of the chair to steady her hands and ignored the annoyed expression Simon gave Anthony. "As we all know, the detective's original theory regarding the death of Charles Woodruff was a simple matter of marital indiscretions gone wrong, but several things that have occurred lately made me question that conclusion and realize that there were indeed several other factors involved."

Pricilla noted the puzzled looks that crossed the faces of her guests and beamed, gaining confidence as she continued to speak. "As we all know, Charles Woodruff was poisoned, but it seems that the case isn't as tied up as everyone once thought. In fact. . ." Pricilla paused for a moment for effect. "It is my belief that the real murderer is right here in this room."

Someone coughed.

Several squirmed in their chairs.

Pricilla kept smiling. It was the reaction she'd hoped for.

"There were plenty of motives among you," she continued, "but the question is, who of the guests, or workers, would stoop low enough for murder? Simon Wheeler and Anthony Mills hated Charles and the fact that he'd taken over their failing business, leaving them bankrupt and giving them both motive and opportunity for the crime. And while Michael hadn't been involved in the actual business dealings, he had invested heavily in the project."

Simon's face turned pale. Anthony gripped his napkin between his fingers like a vise. Michael shoved his chair back from the table. "You can't be serious, Mrs. Crumb. You're accusing us of murder?"

"Not yet. There is also the fact that Charles demanded he be given a new guide this year. For whatever reason, he couldn't stand Oscar." Pricilla watched the guide's jaw tense as her words began to sink in. "It was obvious that the rift between the two men ran deep. Deep enough for one to murder the other, perhaps? And I can't forget the fact that Misty knows far more about the guests than anyone might imagine. I've heard a few of her stories myself. Could something she overheard have led her to murder?"

Apparently, the shock of what she was suggesting had rendered them all speechless, including the real murderer who, up to this point, had thought that he, or she, was getting off scot-free. Now was the moment when she'd bring her rehearsed monologue to a close. With a few well-chosen words, she needed to give the impression that she knew without a doubt who had performed the dreadful deed.

She cleared her throat again and continued. "On the day following Claire's arrest, I discovered a vital clue that made me believe that while Claire might have *intended* to kill her husband, she wasn't the one who administered the final dose that took his life. That, of course, left us with the startling fact that someone other than the victim's wife, someone seated at this very table, was responsible for Charles's untimely demise. And with the evidence piling up, the identity of the antagonist began to take form."

No one moved. The room was silent except for the rain splattering against the widows and the occasional crackle of the fire in the stone hearth. Pricilla turned to each of the guests, one by one, until her gaze finally rested on Max who gave her a subtle smile of encouragement.

A clap of thunder shook the room.

A chair squeaked at the other end of the table. Misty shoved back her seat and let it crash to the floor. "Charles Woodruff paid me to be quiet over the fact that his wife was having an affair." She stumbled toward the door. "But I didn't have anything to do with his murder. I promise. I could never murder anyone."

Someone's fork clanked against the edge of a plate, but no one else spoke. No one else confessed. No one else moved.

Pricilla sat down, numb over the fact that her plan hadn't work. This wasn't what she had envisioned. If Misty was telling the truth and Claire had been the one unfaithful to her husband, then she had the perfect motive to get Charles out of the picture. An uneasy feeling grew in her stomach. What if the detective had been right all along? What if Claire had somehow set up Pricilla, and, in turn, she had played into her hands?

But the woman couldn't have done that.

Or could she?

Others began to rise from the table.

The vein on Simon's neck pulsed as he stopped in front of her. "Your lunchtime interrogation was one thing, but to accuse one of us point blank of murder? This time you went too far."

Michael nodded. "Don't expect us to be back

next year. Your little charade, the clichéd dinner party straight out of the pages of some dusty mystery novel, did you really think it would work?"

Anthony and Oscar said nothing as they walked past. But they didn't have to. Pricilla knew what they were thinking. She had gone too far this time. Those two tiny diuretic pills had ended up causing her a mountain of trouble and, worse, the loss of business for Nathan's lodge.

Max, Nathan, and Trisha stayed to help her pick up what remained of her dignity. Max squeezed Pricilla's shoulder, but even his touch did little to relieve her frustration.

She leaned her elbows against the table and shook her head. "I don't think I've ever been so embarrassed in my life. My grand finale, the clichéd dinner party, as everyone called it, was a total disaster."

"I did try to warn you, Mrs. Crumb." The detective stepped into the room, his ever-present notebook in hand. "There's no doubt in my mind Claire Woodruff killed her husband, and now it looks as if I have even further proof that the lab results will confirm."

Pricilla cringed. The balding officer had been right all along. Nathan had convinced Detective Carter to stand in the wings for the dramatic conclusion, and the confession from the murderer. So much for the theatrics of well-known TV detectives like Dr. Mark Sloan who never had a problem finding out the identity of the murderer.

"What about the person she was having an affair with?" Pricilla knew she was grasping at motives, but if there was any chance to save her self-respect, she'd take it. "We had four capable suspects sitting in this room who might have been involved, and Misty must know—"

"Be assured that while I'm quite certain that Misty's statement will only strengthen the district attorney's case against Mrs. Woodruff, I will follow up on the housekeeper's admission. But, Mrs. Crumb"— the detective shoved his notebook into his back pocket and caught her gaze—"I, as an officer of the law, must advise you to stop making any more attempts to play detective."

Nathan nodded. "He's right, Mom. You've done everything you could. Even I have to agree that it's time you let the sheriff wrap things up."

"I know." Pricilla stood up wishing she could disappear into the polished floorboards. "I think it's time for me to go to bed. All of you were right from the very beginning. I have no business playing the part of a detective. I'm a sixty-four-year-old retiree who needs to find a real hobby."

"Pricilla, you did your best—"

"Don't worry about me. I'm fine." She waved her hand at Max's attempt to comfort her and headed for the hallway.

"Mrs. Crumb?"

Pricilla stopped as Misty entered the room. The

young housekeeper's face was wet with tears.

"I owe you all an apology." Misty glanced at the detective then back to Pricilla. "I didn't mean to cause such a scene, it was just. . .it was just that I was taken by surprise at your remarks, Mrs. Crumb."

"It doesn't matter now." Pricilla shrugged. "The detective will want to talk to you, I know, but I'm the one who should apologize for treating my son's guests as suspects when there was no solid evidence that anyone was guilty. Claire's affair is simply more proof that she's guilty."

"You might be right, but at least let me clear my conscience." Misty took a deep breath and wiped the tears off her cheeks. "What I did was wrong, and it's been bothering me for months. I blackmailed Charles over the fact that his wife was having an affair with Oscar—"

"With Oscar?" Pricilla froze at the name.

Maybe her theory wasn't so far off after all. Claire planned to poison her husband so she could be with Oscar, but if Oscar got impatient. . .

"You were right in what you said about me and my knowing things about the guests." Misty wrung her hands together as she continued, her words breaking into Pricilla's thoughts. "My job lets me find out a lot of things that I'm sure the guests don't want me to know about. Like Claire's affair for one. I never intended to blackmail Mr. Woodruff, but neither did I turn down his generous offer to keep quiet. He told me that her indiscretions might ruin his chances of gaining a political office, something he refused to let happen." She turned to Nathan. "And it isn't at all that I don't appreciate my salary, Mr. Crumb, but I have to think about my children's future, and—"

"We understand, Miss—" The detective cocked his head and waited for an answer.

"Majors. Misty Majors."

"Miss Majors. In the light of your confession, I'm afraid I'm going to have to insist that you come down to the station with me now so I can take a complete statement—"

"Wait a minute." Pricilla's mind was still reeling with Misty's news, but she wondered if she'd done enough damage for one night, or did she dare press the subject further?

"What is it, Mrs. Crumb?" The detective was not smiling.

A truck peeled out of the driveway, and Pricilla caught a glimpse of the dark pickup in the outside lights. The pieces of the puzzle were falling into place. Why hadn't she figured it out before? Shoving her shoulders back, she held her chin high. She had one last attempt to save her reputation.

She turned to the detective. "If Misty's telling the truth, then I believe that the real murderer, Oscar Philips, is making his escape."

Carter ran to the window and shoved back the curtains. Tires spun on the gravel outside the lodge then the pickup raced down the long driveway toward town. Pricilla stared out the darkened window from behind the detective, wondering if Oscar's reaction would prove to be yet another odd twist in the case, or something totally unrelated. She'd never liked Oscar, but that wasn't proof that he'd committed murder. Running from the scene of an investigation, unofficial or not, shined a whole new light on things. Either Oscar had something to hide—like murder—or he had a lot of explaining to do for taking off in such a huff.

The detective addressed Pricilla. "I'm not convinced you're right, Mrs. Crumb, but I'm also not going to take any chances. I'm putting an APB out on Mr. Philips and going after him myself."

Without another word, the detective strode toward the front door and let himself out.

"I'm in shock." Pricilla crossed the room and stared out the window as the detective turned on his lights and sped away from the lodge. "Oscar was never at the top of my list of suspects, though I suppose now he should have been. I'm just having a hard time picturing Claire and Oscar together. What a mess."

Nathan leaned against the back of one of the

chairs. "A very tangled mess."

"Now I feel doubly guilty that I didn't speak up sooner. . .and because of my children, guilty that I did."

A look of fear shot across Misty's face. She sucked in a deep breath and started to hyperventilate. Trisha crossed to the fireplace where Misty stood and put an arm around the woman.

Pricilla fingered the jacquard striped drapery, not feeling quite as sympathetic. "Knowing what you just told us would have tied Claire to Oscar, which would have given him a stronger motive from the beginning."

"And would have explained why Charles was so opposed to Oscar leading the hunt," Nathan added.

"I'm sorry I didn't speak up. I know you're right." Misty leaned back against the stone hearth and sobbed. "The detective's going to arrest me, isn't he? What about my children—"

"I don't know if he'll arrest you." Pricilla laced her fingers behind her back. A part of her did feel sorry for the woman, but withholding evidence had its own consequences. "Since the man you were blackmailing is dead, I don't see why anyone would press charges. And besides, from what you said, it seemed more like he was paying you off rather than you truly blackmailing him."

"I never meant to get involved." Misty wiped her face with her sleeve and headed toward the table. "I'm going to clean up. If the detective returns, you can tell him I'll be in my cabin."

"It looks as if I owe you an apology, Mom," Nathan said as Misty started clearing the table. "Time will tell for certain if you were right, but if I was a betting man, I'd stake my lodge on the fact that Oscar is guilty."

"I agree, but we'll have to wait to find out for sure. While the dinner party didn't bring about the confession I'd hoped for, maybe this is the next best thing." Pricilla shook her head. "In the meantime, I'll make some more coffee. I know I won't be able to get to sleep for a long time."

"I'll help." Trisha followed Pricilla into the kitchen while the men moved into the living room to talk. "I thought the case was closed with Claire's arrest, and now Oscar is mixed up in the whole thing? I just don't get it."

Pricilla pulled a fresh bag of cinnamon hazelnut coffee from the cupboard. "I don't have all the answers at this point, only that Claire definitely wasn't the only one involved. Tonight proved that."

"How about a more pleasant topic for now?" Trisha began filling a wicker tray with coffee mugs. "Tell me what's going on between you and Dad. I can't get over the way he looks at you."

Pricilla felt the heat in her cheeks. Had it really been that obvious? No matter, she knew she deserved the nosy question. She'd certainly asked her fair share of interfering questions in her time, most recently with her attempts to play matchmaker between Trisha and Nathan.

"Is that the motive behind your offer to help?" Pricilla stifled a laugh as she filled the coffee carafe with fresh water. "A chance to find out about me and Max?"

"Not fair." Trisha laughed as she pulled out a stack of saucers and added it to the tray. "But I do admit I've been dying to ask you."

This time Pricilla didn't try to stop the laughter from bubbling out. Not only was laughter a huge relief after the stress of the evening, but she wasn't sure she could suppress her feelings regarding Max any longer.

Pricilla poured the grounds into the filter. "Romance is definitely a more pleasant subject than murder."

"Definitely." Trisha shivered and started setting mugs on a tray. "You don't mind my asking, do you?"

"No. The way I keep secrets, or shall I say the way I don't keep secrets, you were bound to find out sooner rather than later."

"So—" Trisha stopped and faced her.

Pricilla paused. Up until this point, she'd spent the past six hours pondering Max's lunchtime declaration and its consequences. Saying it aloud would make it seem real. Like there was no turning back. Like her life had just changed forever.

Pricilla cleared her throat. "Your father took me out to lunch today, and he brought up the possibility of our relationship growing into something. . .something other than friendship."

"I knew it!" Trisha leaned against the counter and beamed. "And your feelings?"

"I realized that what I felt for him had already begun to change to something beyond friendship, but I hadn't let myself see it."

"And what about the fact that he lives over two hundred miles away?"

Pricilla frowned at the reminder. She wanted to spend the next few days reveling in the fact that Max loved her, not worrying about tomorrow. The Bible was right when it taught that each day had enough trouble of its own. The last few days had certainly had their share.

"I could ask you the same question," Pricilla began. "What about you and Nathan?"

Trisha busied herself with filling the tray with mugs, sugar, and cream.

Pricilla wondered if she'd overstepped her place. "I'm sorry—"

"No." A smile tugged at Trisha's lips. "It's just that I never expected to fall in. . .well, to fall for anyone. Not this quickly anyway."

Pricilla smiled. She'd known from the moment she'd met Marty that he was the one for her, so love at first sight didn't surprise her at all. In her own situation, it might have taken longer with Max for her to discover her true feelings, but she also knew that true love was worth waiting for.

"Sometimes," Pricilla began, "God's timing

surprises us, but if we're in His will, it's always right."

Trisha nodded. "That's exactly how I feel. Like this is God's timing and it's right."

"I just wish all of us lived closer together. I'm not sure I'm up to a long-distance relationship."

Trisha let the pile of teaspoons clank together. "I know that things have moved fast—maybe too fast—between Nathan and me, but I'm thinking about moving to Rendezvous. It would give us a chance to see if things might really work out between us."

Now Pricilla was the one beaming. "I think that's fantastic."

"Really?"

Pricilla squeezed Trisha's hand. "You don't have to seek my approval. You've already got it."

"Thank you." Trisha folded her arms across her chest and faced Pricilla. "I've been building up my online clients for the past year and had planned to quit my day job in the next few months. I could find a small place in town. Neither of us wants to deal with a long-distance relationship. If nothing else, a move like this would give me the push I need to take my graphic design skills to the next level."

Pricilla watched Trisha's animated expression light up her face, and a twinge of reservation swept over her. Trisha was ready to change her entire life for a possible relationship with Nathan. Pricilla wasn't sure she herself was so flexible. How long would it take for her and Max to figure things out between them? How long did it take to adjust to the idea of falling in love the second time around?

The phone on the kitchen wall rang, and Pricilla's heart thudded. All of that was going to have to wait for now because at the moment, there was a far more pressing question at hand. One she hoped to have an answer to tonight. Was Oscar Philips the man guilty of poisoning Charles Woodruff?

        ⸺

While the detective's admission didn't come easily, at eleven o'clock the next morning, he admitted to Pricilla that her theory had been correct. Nathan, busy updating the lodge's Web site and getting a statement ready for the reporters' calls that he knew would be coming, insisted she be the one to announce the authorities' findings to the guests.

Max handed her a mug of black coffee as the guests, along with Misty, filed into the living room. "So you get to play the role of Columbo after all. The brilliant detective whose final monologue lets everyone know, for certain this time, whodunit."

"Except this time the murderer won't be here." She chuckled, warming her hands on the mug with a sigh of relief. No one could be happier than she was that this ordeal was over.

Last night's rain had turned into snow sometime during the night, covering the ground with the white powder that had, in turn, melted this morning, leaving a slushy mess and temperatures that hovered just above freezing. But even the bad weather couldn't dampen her spirits. Oscar was in jail, and the case against him was as solid as the thick wooden beams above her.

"I don't think the detective is quite as thrilled with my sharing the public details of the case as the sheriff is."

Max squeezed her hand. "You deserve it."

She took a sip of the hot drink and watched as Misty slipped into a padded rocker. The normally extroverted housekeeper appeared subdued after spending the morning talking with Detective Carter. She'd obviously learned a thing or two about the merits of minding one's business in her line of work.

Simon, Anthony, and Michael, on the other hand, were full of smiles as they marched into the room and took a seat along the leather couch. While this year's holiday might not have ranked high on their list of top vacations, Nathan's offer to give them a complementary week at the lodge with their spouses, including a four-day hunting trip into the mountains, had obviously soothed their spirits.

Pricilla set her cup down and smoothed the front of her slacks. She made her way to the center of the room, where Detective Carter had addressed them a mere three days ago. It was hard to believe how much had changed in such a short span of time. A man was dead, and the lives of two others destroyed. And in a complete opposite turn of events, she was looking at a future with Max. The thought made her smile and gave her the extra boost of confidence she needed.

The low murmurs in the room silenced as she clasped her hands in front of her. "First of all, I want to apologize to all of you for last night's dinner. I may have seemed a bit overconfident. I'm sorry for contriving the scene. However, it may not have turned out exactly as I intended but in the end, instead of a confession to murder, Oscar was stopped last night a few miles outside of Rendezvous and taken into the sheriff's office for questioning. As the detective explained to me, it didn't take long for the pieces of the puzzle to finally come together and, while there are certainly a few loose ends that will be tied up in the next few days, the sheriff suggested that an update for those involved would be well received."

The fire crackled behind her as she took a step forward onto the multicolored braided rug. "Apparently, when Oscar discovered that Misty knew about his affair with Claire—not to mention the fact that his deed had been announced to the entire group—he panicked, knowing it wouldn't be long until he was tied to the murder of Charles. Though Oscar wasn't at the top of my suspect list, looking back, there were plenty of clues along the way. He mentioned his poor family, and I caught hints of bitterness in his expression as the wealthy dined and vacationed yearly in the lodge. He, in turn, spent his days cleaning the barns and looking after those who never gave him a second glance. The rich wife of one of the guests turned out to be the perfect target.

"Claire only told part of the truth when she mentioned her husband's indiscretions and left out some important details regarding her own. More than likely, Oscar had tried to convince Claire to leave her husband for him in order to gain control of her fortune. When that didn't work, he convinced her to do something more drastic—murder. He must have had an incredible hold on her, but Charles also hadn't been the greatest husband, so Claire was vulnerable. Her attempts to murder her husband, though, didn't work. Instead of poisoning him slowly, the pills she bought turned out to be nothing more than a mild diuretic. With Charles still alive, Oscar got impatient and, blinded by greed, decided to take things into his own hands. He believed that not only would the two of them get away with the deed, but that he'd be set up financially for life."

Pricilla paused in her monologue. "There were other clues. Questions as to why Charles fought with Nathan over the guide. When Charles found out that Oscar would be leading the hunting party, he wanted nothing to do with the man. And knowing his wife was having an affair with the guide was a compelling reason."

She glanced at Misty who was staring at the floor. "Misty's involvement was accidental. When, during last year's hunting trip, Charles found out from Misty that his wife was having an affair with Oscar, he was willing to pay whatever it would take to keep the affair a secret. A divorce would ruin him financially since he'd married Claire for her money, and as a man wanting to go into politics, the affair wouldn't ride well either. There were other things that raised questions throughout the investigation—like the fact that Claire's shoes had been covered with mud from the barn, pointing to the fact that she'd been there to see Oscar.

"The most convincing evidence found so far among Oscar's things was the poison that, in the preliminary testing, matches a substance in the tea Charles drank with my tartlets—a high dose of cyanide extracted from cherry tree leaves. According to the sheriff's investigation, Claire decided to break things off with Oscar after Charles's death because she couldn't stand the guilt in thinking she had killed her husband. Oscar had even been the one to turn up the oven that set off the fire alarm in a desperate attempt to distract everyone so he could talk to Claire.

"And lastly, there are other details of the case, undoubtedly, that won't be released until the trial, but any questions you might have can be addressed to the detective, whom I'd like to thank for following up on my theory despite the fact that he wasn't convinced I was anywhere near the truth."

Pricilla sat down exhausted but relieved that the murder of Charles Woodruff had finally been solved. What Claire did was wrong, and she would still have to deal with the consequences of her actions, but Pricilla promised herself that she would continue to pray that one day Claire would understand the truth that God is good, and that He could forgive her. Perhaps with some help, one day she'd be able to make something of her life again. And the same, she hoped, would be true for Misty as well.

Max ignored everyone else in the room and joined Pricilla on the cushioned love seat, appropriate, she thought, for what she was feeling at the moment.

"I'm proud of you." He ran his thumb down her cheek and smiled. "And now, what do you say we forget about Jessica Fletcher and Columbo and Sherlock Holmes and Dr. Watson and concentrate on us?"

She nodded as he leaned in and kissed her gently on the lips. The newness of his touch left her heart reeling, convincing her that a second chance on love was something worth pursuing.

"I'd like to make a toast—to my mother," Nathan announced to the group, raising his cup of coffee in the air. "For sticking to your convictions, following the evidence, and for being the best novice detective I've ever met."

"Here, here."

"Well done."

She felt the heat rising in her cheeks, something that had been happening far too often lately, and decided that there was only one thing left to say. "Anyone ready for a thick slice of my lemon crumb cake?"

Pricilla Crumb's Recipe for
Lemon Crumb Cake

CAKE:
3 cups flour
3 teaspoons baking powder
¼ teaspoon salt
1 ½ cups butter, softened
3 large eggs + 1 egg white
1 ½ cups sour cream
1 ½ teaspoons lemon zest

CRUMB MIXTURE FILLING:
1 cup flour
½ cup brown sugar, packed
½ teaspoon cinnamon
¼ teaspoon nutmeg
⅓ cup butter, softened

Heat oven to 375°. Coat a 13 x 9-inch baking pan with nonstick cooking spray. Set aside. To prepare the cake, combine flour, baking powder, salt, and butter. Beat on low speed for 30 seconds. Continue beating, adding one large egg at a time, then egg white, sour cream, and lemon zest. Beat another two minutes on medium high.

In a separate bowl, prepare crumb mixture filling by whisking together flour, brown sugar, cinnamon, and nutmeg. Stir in butter until mixture is moistened and starts to stick together.

Pour half of batter into prepared baking pan. Sprinkle crumb mixture filling evenly across the top then cover with remaining cake batter, careful not to mix the filling into the batter. Bake for 30-35 minutes, or until done. Cool completely on a wire rack.

FROSTING:
8 ounces cream cheese, softened
¾ cup unsalted butter, softened
2 cups powdered sugar, sifted before measuring
¼ cup heavy cream
⅓ cup lemon curd

With an electric mixer, blend together: cream cheese, butter, sugar, cream, and lemon curd. When cake is completely cooled, frost and enjoy!

Lisa Harris is a wife, mother, and author who has been writing both fiction and nonfiction for the Christian market since 2000. She speaks French and is learning Portuguese for their current work in Mozambique. Life is busy between ministry and homeschooling, but she loves her time to escape into another world and write, seeing this work as an extension of her ministry. For a glimpse into life in Africa, visit http://myblogintheheartofafrica.blogspot.com or visit her Web site at www.lisaharriswrites.com.

You may correspond with this author by writing:
Lisa Harris
Author Relations
PO Box 721
Uhrichsville, OH 44683

A Letter to Our Readers

Dear Reader:
In order to help us satisfy your quest for more great mystery stories, we would appreciate it if you would take a few minutes to respond to the following questions. We welcome your comments and read each form and letter we receive. When completed, please return to:

Fiction Editor
Heartsong Presents—MYSTERIES!
PO Box 721
Uhrichsville, OH 44683

Did you enjoy reading *Recipe for Murder* by Lisa Harris?

Very much! I would like to see more books like this!
The one thing I particularly enjoyed about this story was:

_____

_____

_____

Moderately. I would have enjoyed it more if:

_____

_____

_____

Are you a member of the HP—MYSTERIES! Book Club?
Yes   No

If no, where did you purchase this book?

_____

Please rate the following elements using a scale of 1 (poor) to 10 (superior):

___ Main character/sleuth   ___ Romance elements

___ Inspirational theme   ___ Secondary characters

___ Setting   ___ Mystery plot

How would you rate the cover design on a scale of 1 (poor) to 5 (superior)? _____

What themes/settings would you like to see in future **Heartsong Presents—MYSTERIES!** selections? _____
_____
_____
_____

Please check your age range:
- ○ Under 18   ○ 18–24
- ○ 25–34   ○ 35–45
- ○ 46–55   ○ Over 55

Name: _____

Occupation: _____

Address: _____

E-mail address: _____

┌─Heartsong Presents—MYSTERIES!─┐

Any 8 Titles
for $32!
A 20%
Savings!

Great Mysteries
at a Great Price!
Purchase Any Title for
Only $4.97 Each!

HEARTSONG PRESENTS—MYSTERIES TITLES AVAILABLE NOW:

__HPM1 *Death on a Deadline*, C. Lynxwiler
__HPM2 *Murder in the Milk Case*, C. Speare
__HPM3 *The Dead of Winter*, N. Mehl
__HPM4 *Everybody Loved Roger Harden*, C. Murphey
__HPM5 *Recipe for Murder*, L. Harris
__HPM6 *The Mysterious Incidents at Lone Rock*, R. K. Pillai
__HPM7 *Trouble Up Finny's Nose*, D. Mentink
__HPM8 *Homicide at Blue Heron Lake*, S. P. Davis & M. Davis

Heartsong Presents—MYSTERIES provide romance and faith
interwoven among the pages of these fun whodunits. Written by the
talented and brightest authors in this genre, such as Christine Lynxwiler,
Cecil Murphey, Nancy Mehl, Dana Mentink, Candice Speare, and
many others, these cozy tales are sure to challenge your mind, warm your
heart, touch your spirit—and put your sleuthing skills to the test.

Not all titles may be available at time of order.
If outside the U.S. please call
740-922-7280 for shipping charges.

SEND TO: **Heartsong Presents—Mysteries** Readers' Service
P.O. Box 721, Uhrichsville, Ohio 44683
Please send me the items checked above. I am enclosing $_____
(please add $3.00 to cover postage per order. OH add 7% tax. WA
add 8.5%). Send check or money order—no cash or C.O.D.s, please.
To place a credit card order, call 1-740-922-7280.

NAME _____

ADDRESS _____

CITY/STATE _____ ZIP_____

HEARTSONG
PRESENTS
MYSTERIES

Think you can outwit clever sleuths or unravel twisted plots?
If so, it's time to match your mystery-solving skills
against the lovable sleuths of
Heartsong Presents—MYSTERIES!

You know the feeling—you're so engrossed in a book that you can't put it down, even if the clock is chiming midnight. You love trying to solve the mystery right along with the amateur sleuth who's in the midst of some serious detective work.

Now escape with brand-new cozy mysteries from *Heartsong Presents—MYSTERIES!* Each one is guaranteed to challenge your mind, warm your heart, touch your spirit—and put your sleuthing skills to the ultimate test. These are charming mysteries, filled with tantalizing plots and multifaceted (and often quirky) characters, but with satisfying endings that make sense.

Each cozy mystery is approximately 250 pages long, engaging your puzzle-solving abilities from the opening pages. Reading these new lighthearted, inspirational mysteries, you'll find out "whodunit" without all the gore and violence. And you'll love the romantic thread that runs through each book, too!

**Look forward to receiving mysteries like this on a regular basis—
join today and receive 4 FREE books with your
first 4 book club selections!**

As a member of the *Heartsong Presents—Mysteries! Book Club*, four of the newest releases in cozy, contemporary, full-length mysteries will be delivered to your door every six weeks for the low price of $13.99. *And shipping and handling is FREE!*

- -

YES! Sign me up for **Heartsong Presents—MYSTERIES!**

NEW MEMBERSHIPS WILL BE SHIPPED IMMEDIATELY!
Send no money now. We'll bill you only $13.99 postpaid with your first
shipment of four books. Or, for faster action, call 1-740-922-7280.

NAME _____

ADDRESS_____

CITY_____ ST_____ ZIP_____

**Mail to: HEARTSONG MYSTERIES,
PO Box 721, Uhrichsville, Ohio 44683
Or sign up at WWW.HEARTSONGMYSTERIES.COM**